Operation Omega

HILARY GREEN

First published in 1984.

This edition published in 2019 by Sharpe Books.

ISBN: 9781096498681

CONTENTS

OPERATION OMEGA

CHAPTER 1

Carlo, the head waiter at La Columbina, was having a quiet evening—that is, until Guy Farnaby punched a reporter on the nose. After that events became what you might call explosive.

Carlo always regarded the appearance of Peter Weatherhead, the gossip columnist, with mixed feelings. On the one hand, Weatherhead tipped lavishly in return for useful information; on the other, he did have a way of occasionally upsetting the restaurant's more sensitive clients. That night he lounged through the main door with the smell of Scotch on his breath and an expression of gloom on his face.

'Who've you got in tonight, Carlo?' he inquired. There's always someone interesting at the Columbina. Don't let me down—it's been a God-awful night so far.'

Carlo scanned the restaurant, playing for time. Of course, there was the party of Arabs dining discreetly in a partly screened off section of the room with some extremely high-powered government officials but Carlo did not think, somehow, that they would appreciate Weatherhead's attentions. He sought for some way of distracting him. Then his eyes lighted on the back of an elegant blonde head and he smiled.

'Leonora Carr is over there, dining with Guy Farnaby.'

'Carr?' Weatherhead looked dubious. 'She's hardly hot news any longer.'

'She is probably still the most beautiful woman in London,' Carlo commented.

'Maybe.' Weatherhead remained unimpressed. 'But it must be getting on for three years since she did that disappearing act from Hollywood, and nearly two since she turned up again in London. People have forgotten the whole story.'

'Forgotten? Forgotten the actress who broke box-office records with one film, the new Garbo, the greatest sex-symbol since Brigitte Bardot?' Carlo was incredulous. 'Not me. I don't forget. Don't you wonder, even now, what made her give the whole thing up and disappear? Don't you wonder why, even now, she refuses all offers to return to films, or to the stage?'

Weatherhead was beginning to look more interested. 'It's a

funny business all right,' he agreed. 'Did you say she was with Guy Farnaby? Now there's another odd character for you. I wonder what she sees in him. "Mystery Star dines with London Playboy"— yes, it might be worth a pic at that. Thanks, Carlo.'

A small wad of notes changed hands and Weatherhead began to make his way casually towards the table which Carlo had indicated. Carlo followed. He wanted to keep an eye on Weatherhead.

The reporter walked almost past the table and then turned quickly back, as if he had just realized who was sitting there.

'Miss Carr? It is Leonora Carr, isn't it?'

Hovering a few feet away Carlo watched her look up and experienced that electric shock to the pit of his stomach which he always felt at the sight of a really beautiful woman. It was the eyes that struck you first, of course, the eyes that had melted the stony hearts of critics all over Europe and America; enormous eyes, of a deep, almost violet blue. Then there was the hair, the colour of pale honey, its long tresses wound and coiled in a style that must have taken some hairdresser hours of work; the purity of the straight nose and the delicate cheekbones; the poise of the pointed chin above the long neck; and perhaps most appealing of all, the sweet curve of the mouth, just a fraction too wide for perfection, which always appeared to be quivering with just-suppressed laughter. The figure, of course, left something to be desired—in Carlo's opinion at least. He did not really care for these slender, northern women. He preferred something more voluptuous; and this girl, really, had breasts that would have seemed small on a child just entering puberty. But still, with those eyes—one could forgive much; anything, indeed.

Weatherhead was saying, 'I hope you don't mind, but I've always been one of your greatest fans…' and the delightful mouth was curving in the beginnings of a courteous smile; not the toothy grin of the star overjoyed at being recognized. But already Farnaby was half-way to his feet…

'Will you please leave us alone! It is really quite intolerable that Miss Carr's privacy should be intruded upon in this way…'

Weatherhead had already produced a tiny camera from his

jacket pocket and was in the process of focusing it. Farnaby went on—

'Put that thing away. We do not wish to be photographed. I insist that you put that thing away at once!'

Carlo saw Leonora's mouth open and her hand raised in a gesture of reason and pacification, but Weatherhead had the camera to his eye and in the same second Farnaby straightened up and let fly with a right hook which seemed out of keeping in its accuracy and power with the suave and fastidious image which he normally liked to present. The camera smashed into Weatherhead's nose and then flew out of his hand as he whirled half round and crumpled onto the floor. Patrons at nearby tables leapt to their feet with cries of anger and alarm and one or two women screamed but Carlo noticed, as he dragged Weatherhead upright, that Leonora was regarding both men with detached, almost clinical curiosity.

In the midst of all the confusion, with Weatherhead swearing and demanding compensation for his camera and Farnaby, in a voice a little too high-pitched to carry authority, insisting that he be removed immediately, Carlo was dimly aware of the party of Arabs making their way towards the door, casting glances of distaste and amazement at the scene. Half his mind registered the fact that he should be there to see them out, to hand coats and umbrellas to the ministers and civil servants who were their hosts. With the other half he was apologizing to Farnaby and hissing in the reporter's ear, 'You go now, yes? Yes, at once! Quick!' as he hustled him towards the door. He reached it just in time to see the Arab party entering the fleet of limousines which had arrived for them. He ejected Weatherhead onto the pavement, ignoring his threats and protests, and hurried back into the restaurant to try and smooth things over with Farnaby.

He was about half-way to the table when something hit him between the shoulder-blades like a battering-ram and sent him sprawling across the dessert trolley. The sound of the explosion, followed by the crash of glass as the windows gave under its force, reached him as he lay there.

It was several seconds before he lifted his head and looked about him. At first it seemed as though the disaster had struck him alone, because looking as he was towards the back of the restaurant he could see no damage, only the shocked faces of the diners as they stared towards him. Then he became aware of a woman screaming, perhaps more than one, a man shouting incoherently, and the crack and tinkle of metal and glass subsiding after being violently wrenched out of place. Slowly he levered himself up off the trolley and turned round. Where the door and the plate-glass windows on either side had been there was now only a jagged-edged space. Between it and himself were overturned tables, twisted steel girders, sharp-edged sherds of glass; and among them men and women, their clothes torn and powdered with grey dust, some of them dragging themselves to their feet, others lying where they had fallen. But it was the sight of what was beyond the windows that drew Carlo's attention. He staggered forward and peered through the smoke and the settling dust. At the edge of the road stood the smouldering remains of the leading limousine. Caught on a sharp edge of metal was a tattered piece of cloth, the remnant of an Arab head-dress. Inside there were shapes, human and yet less than human, from which Carlo's eyes flinched. On the pavement between the car and what had been the door lay a dark bundle. 'How strange,' Carlo thought, 'to leave a dress suit lying in the road—even a tatty old suit like that.' Then he realized that the suit had contained, still contained, the body of Peter Weatherhead.

Police sirens were approaching. Inside the restaurant the uninjured clients were attempting to help the wounded, or struggling across them towards the exit, according to their characters. A movement against the general flow caught Carlo's eye. A slender figure in a blue evening dress moved calmly towards the door at the rear which led to the toilets and the telephones. Thinking that she had mistaken it for a way out of the building and confusedly convinced that he should get everyone out before some new disaster occurred, he followed. In the corridor he found her, speaking calmly into a telephone which some chance had left undamaged. In his dazed condition the words seemed to make very little sense.

'I'm at the Columbina. Tell Pascoe he'd better get down here at once. Sheik Mahoud has just had a rather shattering experience.'

Chapter 2

Ahmed Khalil shook hands with the police inspector who had accompanied him to the door of his local police station. I'm sorry to have dragged you over here for nothing,' the inspector was saying courteously. 'But I'm sure you appreciate that with this latest outbreak of car bombings we have to be seen to be leaving no stone unturned. Purely routine enquiries, you understand.'

'Of course, inspector,' Khalil returned with equal affability. 'The whole business is most regrettable. For those of us who wish to go about our lawful occasions in your country, you will appreciate, it is a grave embarrassment. No-one will be more delighted than we shall when you manage to apprehend these terrorists.'

'Quite so, Mr Khalil,' agreed the inspector. 'Well, thank you again for your co-operation.' 'Not at all,' responded Khalil, 'Anything I can do to help...' and he ran lightly down the steps to the taxi which was waiting for him.

When the taxi drew up outside the block of flats in St. John's Wood where Khalil had been living for the last six months it had to manoeuvre past a post office van which was parked at the kerb with a little protective tent erected behind it over the section of road where the men were working—not that anyone was working, at the time. Khalil paid the taxi and went inside, without noticing the van.

Inside the van a fair-haired man stooped to peer out through the tinted glass of the window.

'There he goes,' he said dispassionately.

His companion, who was seated before a console displaying an array of dials and switches, took up a pair of earphones and turned a knob. He winced and pulled the earphones away from his ears.

'I wish she'd turn that damned tranny off,' he commented.

* * *

Entering his flat, Ahmed Khalil was also surprised for a

moment by the loud pop music issuing from his living-room. Then he remembered that it was Mrs Burkiss's morning. Mrs Burkiss had been hired from a domestic staff agency to clean for him once a week. Normally she came on Thursday, but today she had telephoned with some story about a sister coming to visit and asked if she could come a day early. Khalil swore softly to himself and wished he had not agreed.

He went into the living-room. Mrs Burkiss was dusting energetically at the far end with her back to him. He had to call her name three times before she heard him over the sound of the radio. Then she jumped round looking startled.

'Oh, Mr Khalil, it's you! I thought you'd gone to work.'

'Yes, I had to return unexpectedly—some important papers which I left behind.'

'Oh, what a nuisance for you! Is there anything I can get you? A cup of coffee?'

The voice was a nasal London whine, cockney trying to be genteel. Khalil looked at her with disfavour. He had never cared much for her appearance, but she was efficient and reliable so he had tolerated her. She was a thin, stringy woman, still quite young—a widow with a young son, apparently. In her own misguided way she did her best to make herself attractive, or he supposed that was her idea. Her hair was bleached but always in need of touching up at the roots and she wore glasses with slightly tinted lenses, telling him proudly that the oculist said she was 'photophoberic'. She always used too much make-up and her hands were invariably encased in rubber gloves. In her shapeless overall and down-at-heel shoes she was far from the kind of woman Khalil liked to have about him; and right now he wanted her presence even less than usual.

'Mrs Burkiss,' he said, still having to raise his voice over the radio, 'I have some phone calls to make. I wonder, could you finish this room later?'

'Oh yes, 'course I could,' she exclaimed, with the air of one bestowing a favour. 'I'll go and get on in the kitchen. Just let me know when you've finished, right?'

When she had gathered up her dusters and her radio Khalil stood by the door until he saw her disappear safely into the kitchen. From here, the sound of the music was reassuring. No chance of her accidentally overhearing anything with that row going on, he thought. He went to his desk, picked up the phone and dialled a number.

Down in the van the curly-haired young man with the earphones leaned forward and adjusted a knob.

'Here we go! Thank God she can't drown this with her radio!'

His partner leaned over him and he held one earphone away from his head so that they could both hear the conversation. In front of them a tape-recorder began to turn as the ringing-tone was answered.

'Farnaby,' said the voice at the end of the line.

'Mr Farnaby.' Khalil's voice was suave and unruffled. 'It is Ahmed Khalil here. I am sorry to bother you but I am afraid I shall have to cancel our appointment. I have to go away for a few days, on business, you understand.'

'Away?' queried Farnaby sharply.

'For a few days only,' Khalil said soothingly. 'I will telephone you when I return. But let me assure you that the delivery of the goods you have ordered will not be affected in any way.'

'You're sure about that?'

'Quite sure. The goods will be delivered exactly according to schedule. You may rely on that.'

'Oh well, that's all right then.' Farnaby sounded reassured. 'I'll wait for you to get in touch with me then…'

'Yes, yes. In a few days. Until then...'

'Yes, right. Until then. Goodbye.'

Khalil put the phone down and unlocked a drawer in his desk. His movements were not in keeping with the calm tone which he had used to Farnaby. Swiftly he sorted the papers in the drawer into two piles. One he put into his brief-case. The other, after a moment's thought, he placed in a plastic carrier-bag which he found in the hallway. Nobody would notice a plastic carrier dumped somewhere, whereas a fire in a modern, centrally heated flat... He stooped to check that nothing had been left at the back of the drawer and as he did so his eye was caught by something under the edge of the desk. He reached out and withdrew a small metal object about the size of a button.

For a few moments he sat absolutely still, gazing at it, absorbing the implications, his mind racing as he tried to work out how it had come there. Then his lips tightened and he gave a small jerk of his head. He opened a small drawer, searched in it for a moment and took out a business card on which was printed THE CAVENDISH DOMESTIC AGENCY and an address in Knightsbridge.

After a further moment's thought Khalil took out a note pad and an envelope. He wrote briefly, in Arabic script, and then put the letter and the card into the envelope and inscribed on it an address in Clapham. Then he got up and went to the window which looked out onto the street. This time he did see the post office van.

Soft-footed, he crossed the room and looked out into the hall. The radio was still playing loudly in the kitchen. He slipped silently out of the front door, leaving it ajar behind him, and ran down one flight of stairs to the flat below. For a moment he was afraid that there would be no answer to his ring on the doorbell, but then he heard feet approaching. The door was opened by a heavily built woman with blue-rinsed hair and several diamond rings on her fat fingers. Khalil smiled his most charming smile.

'Mrs Pemberton, I am so sorry to disturb you, but I wonder if I could ask you a great favour.'

The woman smiled at him expansively. 'Mr Khalil! There's no need to apologize! We don't see nearly enough of you. Do come in, won't you?'

'Thank you, no,' Khalil murmured. 'You see, I am not feeling very well. I think it may be the flu, and I don't want to pass it on to you or your family. That is why I want to ask you a favour.'

'Well, of course,' the woman exclaimed. 'If you're poorly we'll be only too glad to help. What can I do for you?'

'This letter—' Khalil held up the envelope,—'it's absolutely vital that it should reach its destination today. I was going to deliver it myself but I really don't feel up to it. I was wondering—your son is at home?'

'Frank? Yes, he's here. College doesn't start again for a week yet.'

'And he still has his motor bike?'

'Motor bike? Oh, yes, of course! Now I'm with you. He's done little messages for you before, hasn't he. He'll deliver your letter, no trouble at all. Just give it to me. I'll see he goes off with it straight away.'

Khalil handed over the letter and with it a five-pound note.

'A little something to pay for the petrol, you understand,' he murmured.

Then, waving aside Mrs Pemberton's offers to call a doctor or fetch him aspirins et cetera, he made his way swiftly back up to his flat. The radio still played in the kitchen. Ahmed Khalil went into the living-room and picked up the small metal object. Then he went into the kitchen. Mrs Burkiss was scouring the sink and did not see him come in. Still moving quietly he crossed the room and turned the radio up to full volume.

Down in the post office van the young man with the earphones swore.

For the second time that morning Mrs Burkiss turned round with a start to face her employer. He moved to within a few paces of her and spoke softly but very distinctly. 'Mrs Burkiss, do you know what I have just found on my desk?'

She was staring at him, wide-eyed. 'Found, Mr Khalil?'

He held up his hand, the fist lightly clenched. 'Yes, Mrs Burkiss. A bug, that is what I have found. And now I want to know how it got there.'

'A bug!' She goggled at him. 'Oh, Mr Khalil, I'm ever so sorry. I can't think how it got there.' Her mouth opened and shut as she sought for words. 'What sort of a bug, Mr Khalil?' Then, with something like a giggle, 'Ooh, do take it away! I can't stand creepy- crawlies!'

Khalil stared at her. If this was pretence, she was a very fine actress. But yet how else…? He stepped closer and opened his hand under her nose.

'Not a creepy-crawly, Mrs Burkiss. This! You know quite well what this is, don't you. Now tell me who told you to plant it—and where are the rest of them?' She was gazing at him in silence now, like a hypnotized rabbit. He pressed home his advantage. 'Tell me about the agency that sent you here. Did somebody there tell you to plant these on me? What is the Cavendish Staff Agency, really? Who exactly do you work for?'

He moved closer still as he spoke so that she was pressed back against the sink, her hands stretched out on either side of her. He saw the rather wide, over-lipsticked mouth working in silent terror and smiled at the thought that he would not have too much difficulty in getting the information he wanted. Then the world exploded around him in agony as Mrs Burkiss brought her knee up and caught him with merciless accuracy in the crotch. He doubled up, gasping, and as he did so the pain was swallowed up in sudden darkness as the edge of her hand came down on his neck in a karate chop that would have felled an all-in wrestler.

Mrs Burkiss looked down at the prostrate figure at her feet for a moment. Then she bent and pulled him over onto his back. With rapid, impersonal movements she pulled back an eyelid, checked the pulse at his throat and then went through the contents of his pockets. Her investigation completed she rose and went to the holdall which she always carried with her. She delved beneath the folded mac and the extra cardigan and produced a pair of handcuffs; then, taking Khalil by the wrists, she dragged him over to the leg of a peninsula unit which was firmly screwed to the floor and handcuffed him to it. Then she went into the living-room and sat down at the desk to glance through the papers in the two bags. Finally, she returned to the kitchen and switched off the radio.

Down in the van the operator sighed with relief and took up the earphones again. A voice came over them, clear to both men. 'OK. Send in the clowns . . .' The tone was relaxed, almost weary; but it was not the nasal cockney of Mrs Burkiss. It was a melodious, expressive voice, an instrument perfectly trained to its owner's purposes. The two men in the van exchanged glances which combined surprise and appreciation. The voice went on, 'Mr Khalil has been unavoidably detained. You'll find him in the kitchen. But there's no need to hurry. "He will stay till you come".'

'Shakespeare yet!' muttered the curly-haired one, who was a young man of some education. His companion grunted.

'But who the hell was that?' he asked.

Chapter 3

The Spartacus Health Club provided excellent facilities for its members, right in the heart of London's West End. There was a swimming- pool, a gymnasium, a sports hall, squash courts and all the usual adjuncts of saunas, solarium and so forth. Very few of the members realized, however, that the top two floors of the building housed a very different organization, which was, in its own way, also dedicated to the health of the community, though from a very different standpoint. The Special Security Service, known to those who knew of its existence at all as the Triple S—or to some of its less ardent admirers as the Snake Pit—was officially a department of the Home Office, working in close co-operation with the police. In practice, under its commander, James Pascoe, an ex-cop himself, it was an autonomous organization answerable only to the very highest authority.

The inspiration, which had been his own, to build the Health Club as a cover for the organization gave Pascoe a good deal of quiet satisfaction. It enabled his operatives to come and go without any danger of revealing their connection with the service, provided first-class training facilities in the private suite on the fourth floor and gave him an ideal apartment where he could literally live on the job. He had long ago given up making the effort to go back to what was still officially his home in Surrey, except for the occasional weekend. It also meant that he could indulge his own passion for keeping fit whenever he had a spare half-hour.

It was a source of mild regret to him that very few of his hand-picked and highly trained agents appreciated his own favourite sport of fencing, most of them preferring the more violent martial arts to the sublety and finesse of the foil or the épée. There was one, however, who could give him a match, one who realized that speed and perfect co-ordination could overcome brute force; and on that particular Thursday morning Pascoe was enjoying a specially lively and well-balanced bout. Advance and retire, parry, riposte and lunge; the body in perfect balance, the fingers alone guiding the flickering point of the foil, his eyes fixed on the slight figure of his opponent—a slender enough target, even in the padded fencing jacket. He tried to stare past the mask, fancying that he caught the glint of blue eyes through the close mesh and, for an instant, his concentration must have wavered; feint, parry, *doublé*, *trompé*, *dégagé* and lunge. The point of the foil fixed itself into his jacket just above the heart and the blade arced upwards in a supple curve.

'Touché!' Pascoe acknowledged.

His opponent recovered from the lunge in a single lithe movement and the foil blade swept up and then sideways in salute.

'My bout, I think.'

Pascoe returned the salute gravely and pulled off his mask, smiling at the flushed cheeks and rumpled honey-coloured curls of the girl who faced him.

'You're getting too good for me!'

'Nonsense,' she returned crisply. 'You let me win sometimes, just so I don't get discouraged and give up all together.'

'You know that isn't true,' he returned, 'because it isn't necessary. Listen, I want to talk to you. Come up when you've showered and have breakfast with me.'

She nodded. 'Fine.'

I'll give you fifteen minutes.'

The girl grinned. 'Make it ten. I'm a working girl, remember. I have to be in the office by nine.'

He laughed. 'Have it your own way.' Promptly ten minutes later she walked into the room which Pascoe used as an office by day and a sitting-room outside working hours. Dressed now in beautifully fitting jeans and a silk shirt she hardly looked, Pascoe thought in passing, like your typical office girl. Over the second cup of coffee he said,

'Right, business. Tell me about yesterday.' His companion grimaced over her cup. 'Sorry about that. I know you didn't intend to pick Khalil up so soon; but he found one of the bugs and somehow made the connection with the agency. I couldn't risk him passing that information on to anyone else.'

'You were absolutely right,' Pascoe told her. 'The agency is far too valuable as a cover to risk having it blown. Anyway,

Khalil was obviously on his way out of the country. We should have to have had him picked up within a matter of hours at the airport, or wherever he was headed. We got what we really wanted from him.

'You mean the telephone conversation with Farnaby?'

'Yes. Have you heard the tape?'

She nodded. 'Cindy played it over to me in Control when I looked in yesterday evening.'

'It's not enough on its own, of course,' Pascoe went on. 'But at least it proves that we're not barking up the wrong tree. The connection between Khalil and Farnaby does exist.'

'And Farnaby is expecting a delivery of some sort in the near future.'

'If only we knew exactly when—and where,' Pascoe mused. 'How are things progressing on that front?'

'I think we're making progress.' His companion put down her cup and leaned forward. 'Farnaby is giving a big party on Saturday night down at his country house in Hampshire. You know he's got a place right on the Hamble estuary? If he is bringing drugs in, that could be the ideal place to land them. Also, I suspect that it's at do's like this he selects his victims. He's a very choosy pusher, our friend Farnaby. You have to be extremely well-connected to get on his books. I reckon he invites the cream of local "society" to a house party—either down in Hampshire or at his place in town—and picks out the kids who look daft enough, or vulnerable enough, to be useful to him. After he's got them hooked— well, he's got not only them but Mummy and Daddy on the end of a piece of string.'

'It's a good theory,' Pascoe agreed, 'but can we get any hard evidence?'

'That's what I'm hoping to do this weekend.'

'You're going to the party?'

'Yes. I think Farnaby's decided that I might be a potential customer.'

Pascoe sighed and shook his head. 'I don't like it, you know. You're going right out on a limb, completely on your own. If something went wrong…'

She shook her head. 'Nothing will go wrong, James. Why

should it? As far as Farnaby is concerned I'm just a washed-up ex-actress and full-time junkie who makes a pretty bit of window-dressing.'

Pascoe looked at her. 'I don't like to hear you speak of yourself in that disparaging tone,' he said quietly.

The remarkable blue eyes returned his gaze with a level, ironic stare. 'What, about the girl they once called "the thinking man's Marilyn Monroe"?'

Pascoe's normally austere face softened. 'I prefer to remember her as the actress the critics acclaimed as the greatest Rosalind of her generation.'

For a moment her eyes dropped. 'Ah,' she said softly, 'but that was in another country and besides…'

'And besides, the wench is dead,' he finished for her. 'But she isn't, is she? And I want to make sure it stays that way. I wish you'd let me give you some back-up for this operation.'

'But can't you see, James,' she exclaimed, 'that that is the worst thing you could do? The less connection there is between me and Triple S the better.' She smiled at him. 'Don't worry. Everything'll be fine. I've got to go now. Bad example for the boss to come in late, you know.'

She rose, picked up a denim jacket and a holdall and went to the door. 'Bye, James. See you tomorrow.'

'Bring your foil,' he said. 'I want my revenge.' Then, as she opened the door, 'Take care now.'

She smiled, put her fingertips to her lips and blew the kiss towards him.

* * *

At the same instant the doors of the private lift at the end of the corridor leading to Pascoe's apartment opened to let out the two men who had been on duty in the post office van outside Khalil's flat. Seeing the girl in the doorway, the gesture of the blown kiss, they paused and exchanged looks of surprise and amusement. Pascoe was not in their experience the sort of man one imagined people blowing kisses to. As they walked on the girl came towards them, heading for the lift. They both stood aside to let her pass between them and as she did so their eyes swept over her with frank appreciation. Marriot, the younger one with the curly hair, noticed the lithe walk, the bounce of the honey-coloured hair and the cool poise of the chin. Stone, his partner, working from the ground up, saw the long legs, the slender waist, the wide, amused mouth and, with a faint shock, blue eyes which met his own with something that felt like a challenge. Then she was past them, walking away, and leaving him with his eyes glued to the neatest bottom he had ever seen inside a pair of jeans. They moved on, towards Pascoe's door, and Stone heard Marriot knock and the answering 'Come in'. Marriot opened the door and courteously waved him through. The girl had reached the lift and was waiting for the doors to open. Stone turned, and walked smartly into the doorpost.

Nick Marriot, looking back and struggling to suppress his laughter, saw the girl turn inside the lift just in time to observe his partner's mishap and thought he saw, as the doors closed, the lips twitch into an irrepressible grin.

* * *

A neat, white TR7 drew up in the Knightsbridge mews which housed the offices of the Cavendish Domestic Agency. In the parking slot labelled LEC stood a rather dilapidated red Mini. The driver of the TR7 wound down the window and peered at it with some annoyance, then parked neatly across its tail, got out, locked the car and ran upstairs to the agency's offices on the first floor.

In the outer office a dark-haired woman in her forties was checking a file cabinet, a blonde was typing and a fresh-faced, plump girl of 17 or 18 was going through the morning's mail. The owner of the TR7 paused in the doorway.

'There's a nasty little red car in my parking slot.'

The plump girl scrambled to her feet, her cheeks reddening.

'Oh, Miss Cavendish, I'm terribly sorry! It's mine. I didn't realize that was your place.'

'Didn't you see the notice—LEC?'

'Oh yes, I saw it. I thought it was something to do with the

London Electricity Board.'

The figure in the doorway leaned one hand on the doorpost in a theatrical gesture.

'L.E.C.' she intoned. 'Laura Eleanor Cavendish! Electric I maybe, sweetheart, but bored, never!'

'I'm sorry,' the girl repeated. 'I'll go and move it.'

Laura Cavendish straightened up. 'There's a good girl,' she said briskly. 'Here.' She tossed some keys across to the girl's desk. 'You'll have to shift mine first. I'm parked right across your tail. Irene, can you come through, please. I want to go over next week with you.'

The dark-haired woman followed her into the inner office. When the door had closed behind them the girl said,

'Do you think she was really angry?'

'Good lord, no,' replied the blonde. 'Laura doesn't get angry about little things like that, thank God.'

The girl looked after her employer wistfully. 'I wish I looked like that in jeans!'

'Don't we all!' said her colleague. 'Still, I suppose if we had the energy and the self-discipline to go to a health club every morning before work, and dance classes twice a week in the lunch hour, we probably would.'

In the inner office Laura was saying, 'Is that new girl as gormless as she appears?'

Irene, the office manager, laughed. 'No, not really. She's quite bright, and very willing. I think she finds you rather overpowering, that's all.'

'What's in the post today?' Laura asked.

'Jenny's sorting it now,' Irene told her. 'I expect she'll be in with it as soon as she's moved your car.'

'Did you hear any more…' The question was cut short as the glass in the window was shattered by an explosion. Irene flung herself to the floor with her hands over her ears. It was Laura who reached the shattered window within seconds and looked out. Below, in the mews, her TR7 stood untouched on the opposite side of the road. In the parking spot labelled with her initials the remains of a red Mini could be seen through a dense cloud of oily smoke.

Chapter 4

Peter Stone was not happy in his work. If there was one thing that was guaranteed to annoy him, it was the feeling that he was being used as a baby-minder.

'If you ask me,' he said, swinging the car rather more viciously than necessary round a right-hand corner, 'Pascoe's lost his marbles.'

Nick Marriot looked up from the A-Z on his lap. It did not need the sight of his partner's set jaw and the hard line of his mouth to tell him his mood. He could feel the tension exuding from the compact, muscular body.

'How's that?' he asked casually.

'Hasn't he got any better use for us than acting as nursemaids to one of his ex-girlfriends?' Stone demanded.

'What makes you think she's an ex-girlfriend?'

'"Miss Laura Cavendish is a close friend of mine. I should be very distressed if anything were to happen to her"!' Stone had a talent for mimicry and his voice caught exactly the languid ex-public-school accent of his superior. Then, in his own voice, 'I didn't join this outfit to run round after middle-aged ladies with a nervous disposition.'

'She did get her car blown up this morning,' Nick pointed out.

'Correction. Somebody else's car that happened to be in her parking slot got blown up. What makes her think the bomb was intended for her?'

'Pascoe must think it was,' Nick commented reasonably. 'Anyway,' he was glancing through a file of papers on his knee, 'What makes you so sure she's middle-aged?'

'Got to be, hasn't she,' Stone said firmly. 'Look at the file. Head of a domestic agency with offices in Knightsbridge; home address a flat in Chelsea. How many dolly-birds do you know who can run to that sort of life-style? I'll bet you that she's a middle-aged battle-axe with a cut-glass accent and a Maggie Thatcher hair-do.'

Nick looked interested. 'Usual terms?' he asked.

'Done!' replied Stone.

'Incidentally,' Nick commented. 'According to this she drives a TR7. That doesn't quite seem to fit with your image.'

'Trying to be trendy. Doesn't want to admit she's past it.' Stone's voice was crisp and confident. 'I know the type.'

'Take the next right,' Marriot told him. 'It's a one-way street.'

Stone pulled over to the centre of the road and was about to swing across into the mews when a white TR7 shot out of it, swerved across his nose and roared away up the main road. Stone caught a glimpse of a slight figure wearing denims and a cap pulled down above dark glasses.

That's her car!' yelped Marriot.

'Sure as hell isn't her driving it!' Stone returned as he dragged the wheel of the Capri over and headed in pursuit, cutting up a double-decker bus as he did so.

The TR7 turned out into Sloane Street and headed south, moving fast in the relatively light afternoon traffic. Stone closed up behind. The TR7 took a sharp right into Cadogan Gardens.

'Reckon he's spotted us,' commented Marriot.

As if to prove his point the car ahead suddenly swerved right again, without giving a signal, cutting across the nose of an on-coming taxi and forcing it to slam on its anchors so sharply that the passenger was almost catapulted into the front seat. The driver jumped out but his flood of abuse was abruptly stifled when Stone almost ran over his toes as he screamed past.

This road was quieter, with little approaching traffic. Stone accelerated and drew level with the TR7. Marriot wound down his window and waved the driver into the kerb. The white car slowed and eventually came to a standstill just beyond a side turning. Stone pulled in ahead.

'Some kid, joy riding,' Stone grunted as he got out. 'I'll sort him…'

They walked back towards the TR7. As soon as they were clear of their own car the driver started the engine again and reversed smartly past the turning. Marriot ran forward with a yell and barely escaped being mown down as the car leaped forward and accelerated hard into the side-road. By the time they had regained the Capri and Stone, swearing softly but extremely comprehensively, had reversed it and set off once again in pursuit, the white car was already disappearing round the corner at the far end of the street. Pedestrians turned to stare as the Capri snarled down the road and shot the lights at the junction just as they turned to red.

For a moment they thought that they had lost the TR7 completely until they came in sight of it standing by the kerb outside South Kensington station. A slight figure in blue denims was just disappearing inside. Stone skidded to a halt and they leaped out and raced into the station, brushing past a protesting ticket-collector as they headed for the escalators. There were few people about and they had an uninterrupted view of the escalator ahead as they pounded down it, but there was no sign of their quarry. However, towards the bottom they passed a girl, gliding upwards, a girl with honey-coloured hair, dressed in jeans and a silk shirt and carrying a navy holdall. Both experienced a sudden twinge of recognition, but their minds were on other things.

When they reached the platforms they heard the sound of a train pulling out and were just in time to see its rear lights disappearing into the tunnel. They split up and made a swift survey of both platforms but there was no one on either of them who remotely resembled the person they were seeking. Meeting again at the bottom of the escalator they exchanged looks and shrugged.

'Damn!' said Stone succinctly.

As they floated up Marriot said,

'That girl we passed on the way down ...'

'Yeah,' said Stone. 'Seen her before somewhere.'

'Wasn't she the girl we saw coming out of Pascoe's room this morning?'

Stone snapped his fingers. 'That's it. Knew I'd seen her before somewhere.'

There was a pause. Then Marriot said, 'Funny that.'

'Yeah,' Stone agreed again. 'Odd.'

They reached the street level and waved their warrant cards at the irate collector.

'Well, at least we've got the car,' Stone commented.

Marriot looked up and down the road.

''Fraid not,' he said.

The TR7 was just disappearing round the corner.

'I don't believe it!' Stone groaned.

Marriot touched his arm and jerked his head.

'You're not going to believe this either.'

Over by the kerb a traffic warden was affixing a ticket to the windscreen of Stone's car.

* * *

In the window of her first-floor flat looking out on a quiet square between the King's Road and the river Leonora was talking on the telephone, with more than a hint of annoyance in her voice.

'James? It's Leo. Listen, I've just been chased across London by two of your heavies.'

Pascoe's voice was jolted for a moment out of its usual even tones. 'What do you mean— chased?'

'Chased, James—as in pursued!' Leonora was simulating a little more anger than she actually felt. 'Do you want me to spell it for you?'

'Are you sure they were my men?'

'Of course they were your men! I haven't been around Triple S this long without getting to know those two by sight. Your wonder boys—Tweedledum and Tweedledee— Batman and Robin…'

'You mean Stone and Marriot,' Pascoe remarked dryly.

'That's it,' she agreed. 'I told you I knew them.'

'Leo,' he said soothingly, 'they weren't chasing you. Their instructions were to keep an eye on you—from a discreet distance.'

'Well,' Leo commented, 'I don't know how you interpret that, James, but would you say it included forcing me off the road and chasing me into a tube station?'

'They what?' Pascoe exclaimed. 'Where are they now?'

'I lost them at South Ken. With any luck they're still going round and round on the Circle Line.'

Pascoe recovered his self-control. 'Look, Leonora, there's

been some mistake—a misunderstanding...'

'You're too right there has!' she cut in. 'James, I told you quite specifically that I didn't want any protection. I'm perfectly safe as long as Farnaby can't connect me with Triple S, but how long is that going to last with the Lone Ranger and Tonto thundering around behind me?' She looked out of the window. A bronze Capri had just drawn up on the opposite side of the street. 'Oh-oh! You know what I said about going round on the Circle Line? Well, they're not. They've just driven up outside. James, did you give them my home address?'

'Of course I did,' he said reasonably. 'Now listen, Leo, I don't know what went wrong but I'm going to find out. I'll have them recalled straight away.'

Leo was gazing speculatively at the two men in the car. 'No, don't bother, James,' she murmured. 'On second thoughts, if they are going to be around we might as well get to know each other. Get Control to call them and tell them to come up and introduce themselves, will you?'

Back in his flat above the health club Pascoe smiled to himself.

'That's a good girl! I knew you'd see the sense of it. I'll get a message through to them straight away.' Then, as she was about to put the phone down, 'Oh—by the way, Leo...?'

'Yes, James?'

'Er—which one is Batman, would you say?'

Leo grinned and looked out of the window. 'Oh, I couldn't possibly tell you, James—yet. I'll let you know—in due course.'

She replaced the phone and stood watching the two men. They had got out of the car and seemed undecided about whether to come across to the flat or stay where they were. Yes, she had been right about their identities. Pascoe's top two agents. She supposed she should be flattered. They were the two she had met outside Pascoe's apartment that morning. The fair, tough-looking one was Stone. She remembered the encounter in the corridor and recalled a pair of ice-blue eyes which had glinted with the tacit assumption that any girl Stone found attractive must automatically return the compliment. She had to admit he had some grounds for his self-confidence—if you happened to fancy the hard, Nordic type— but the realization had lent an extra spice to her enjoyment when she saw him walk into that door post. The other one, now, the tall, loose-limbed one with the curly hair—that was Marriot. They were an oddly contrasted pair. Marriot, with his long hair and his faded jeans, could have walked out of any coffee bar, or any building site; but she remembered warm, hazel eyes with a thick fringe of dark lashes, which had met her own with friendly, open approval. She watched him standing, leaning on the roof of the car—very laid-back; very relaxed. Stone stood still too, but his stillness was the repose of a coiled spring, balanced, alert; not restful. The roll-necked sweater and the leather jacket were the clothes of a man who cared about the way he looked and was prepared to spend money on it. A hard man, Stone, she thought, smiling at the pun. Rock-hard? Or harder? She recalled the glint in the pale blue eyes. Diamond-hard, perhaps. The idea pleased her. Yes, a diamond—but a rough diamond, if her guess was right.

She saw him bend suddenly and unhook the microphone of the car radio. Control had obviously come through with Pascoe's message. Smiling, she turned away from the window and went across to the navy holdall which stood by her desk.

A couple of minutes later, having been admitted by the remote-control lock on the front door, Stone and Marriot walked somewhat warily into the hallway of the flat.

'In here,' called a voice.

Stone pushed open the door which stood ajar and looked across the room. Seated behind the big desk in the window, silhouetted against the strong light from outside, was the slim figure in the cap and denim jacket which they had pursued that afternoon.

It was Nick Marriot who stepped forward.

'Miss Laura Cavendish?'

The girl behind the desk reached up and removed the cap, allowing her hair to fall round her face.

'It's Leonora, actually. Laura is just a business name.'

Marriot, his eyes accustoming themselves to the light, put his hand behind him where Stone could see it and made grasping motions with it. He had not forgotten their bet. Stone, however, ignored it. He was beginning to have a most unpleasant feeling that he had been made a monkey of.

'It was you driving the TR7,' he said brusquely.

'Why not?' Leo replied sweetly. 'It's my car.'

'And you who passed us on the escalator,' said Marriot, beginning to smile.

'I'm afraid so,' she grinned back at him.

'And you we saw leaving Pascoe's room this morning.'

'Right again.'

Stone interrupted this growing rapport. 'So what the hell are we playing at?' he demanded.

Leo lowered her chin and eyed him coldly. 'What the hell were you playing at, forcing me off the road?'

Stone moved forward to the desk. 'Look, you came out of that one-way street like a bat out of hell. How were we to know it was you driving?'

Enlightenment dawned on Leo's face. 'Oh, now I get it! You thought I'd pinched the car.'

'Well, you must admit it looked a bit—odd,' Marriot murmured.

Leo sat back in her chair. 'OK. Fair enough. I owe you an explanation. I was half-expecting someone to follow me. There had been a strange car parked outside the office for an hour before I left, with a guy sitting in it. I figured if he was waiting for me the easiest way to give him the slip was to come out the wrong way. Of course, when I realized you two were on my tail I assumed you were part of the same outfit.' She paused, and grinned. 'It's a good job there weren't any coppers around.'

Marriot returned her smile. He was completely captivated. Stone, however, was not.

'Look,' he said. 'I don't know whether you realize it, but we are members of the police force.'

'Ah,' said Leo softly, 'but not that sort of police.'

Stone drew out his warrant card and thrust it under her nose. 'Special Security Service.'

If he had expected Leo to be impressed he was disappointed. She glanced at the ID, then lifted her eyes and looked from him to Marriot and back.

'Look.' she said, 'I think we've all got off on the wrong foot. Let's start again.' She rose and came round the desk. 'I'm Leonora Cavendish. Who are you?'

'Sorry,' Marriot said quickly. 'I'm Nick Marriot.'

He took her proffered hand. It was firm in his own, but very small. She looked at Stone, who glowered in return.

'He's Stone,' Marriot said.

Leo turned to him and offered her hand again. 'Stone, *tout court*? she queried.

Stone shook it briefly. 'Yes—except to particularly close friends.'

Leo acknowledged the barb with a lift of her eyebrows and turned away.

'I think we could all use a drink. Is Scotch OK?'

'Fine, thanks,' agreed Marriot.

'Sit down,' Leo said, pouring drinks. 'Make yourselves comfortable.'

Marriot dropped into an easy chair and looked around him. It was a big room, high-ceilinged with long windows. The décor was mainly shades of cream and fawn, with touches of clear, pale blue, against which the rich mahogany and rosewood of a few pieces of beautiful old furniture glowed warmly. There was very little ornament except for one or two pieces of Wedgwood and crystal. The effect was cool, elegant and yet very relaxing.

Leo handed him a glass and then gave one to Stone, who had seated himself on a upright chair by the desk.

'Cheers,' she said, knocking back a mouthful of Scotch in a straightforward, business-like manner which Nick found reassuring.

'Cheers,' he replied. Stone drank in silence, but his eyes never left her.

'Right!' said Leo. 'No more games. I didn't want you on this case but now you're here I suppose you'll be less of a nuisance if I put you in the picture.'

Marriot glanced at his partner's face. It was a study. This was simply not the way women were supposed to behave towards Stone— particularly attractive women.

Leo leaned across the desk and reached into a drawer to extract a slim black wallet. She handed it to Stone.

'Snap!'

Stone looked at the Triple S ID card in silence and handed it on to Marriot, who chuckled delightedly.

'I should have guessed.'

'OK.' said Stone truculently. 'So what's the idea? Why didn't Pascoe tell us this to start with?'

Leo seated herself on the edge of the desk. 'I'm afraid that was my fault. You see, the whole point of the way I operate is that I have as little visible connection with Triple S as possible.'

'And this Cavendish Agency is your cover?' Marriot put in.

'One of them, yes. It's a genuine domestic staff agency too, of course, but you'd be surprised how many "interesting" houses you can get into as a cleaner, or a cook or a nanny.'

'So what are you involved with at the moment?' Nick asked.

'You know about Ahmed Khalil?'

'We picked him up yesterday.'

'Oh?' Leo smiled. 'It was you in the van, was it?'

'Yes. How...?' Recognition dawned on Nick's face. 'Mrs Burkiss!'

Leo laughed. 'Yes, her too.'

'Dear God!' muttered Stone.

Leo went on. 'Does the name Guy Farnaby mean anything to you?'

'Playboy, man-about-town type.' Stone was beginning to be interested in spite of himself. 'Always getting his photo in the papers with expensive women. Was there a rumour about drugs once?'

'That's him,' agreed Leo. 'The original playboy of the western world. Ex-Eton, well- connected, well off—too well off for his visible sources of income. Likes to be seen as a patron of the arts, but also operates in that shady area where big money and influence mix and nobody asks too many questions. We're pretty sure that he's pushing dope to what you might call the "gilded youth" of society—kids with plenty of money on the look out for the latest kicks.'

'How does he connect with Khalil?' Nick asked.

'Well, you heard his last phone call. It was to Farnaby. That more or less confirms our suspicions. Khalil is supplying Farnaby, in order to raise money for terrorist operations— and in return for some other very useful perks.'

'Such as?' queried Stone.

'Well, think of the circle Farnaby moves in. Look at the potential for blackmail when he's supplying the sons and daughters of politicians, industrialists, the aristocracy— maybe even judges and senior police officers. A bit of information here, somebody leaned on there—very useful for Farnaby, even more useful for Khalil.'

'Can you prove this?' Stone asked.

'If I could we wouldn't be sitting round here now, would we?' Leo asked. 'That's the next step. Farnaby likes to be seen around with attractive women. It's a matter of window dressing really. He's actually rather heavily involved with a very beautiful boy from the *corps de ballet* at the moment. That's where the other me comes in.'

'The other you?' queried Marriot.

Leo reached into the desk again and produced a framed photograph. It was a Hollywood publicity still, very glossy and glamorous. She held it out to them.

'Does this ring any bells?'

Marriot and Stone stared at the picture for a long moment in silence. Then Nick said slowly,

'No wonder I kept thinking I'd seen you somewhere before this morning!'

'Leonora Carr!' muttered Stone. 'I must be losing my grip or something.'

'I shouldn't worry about it,' Leo said. 'It was a long time ago.'

'Can't be more than a couple of years,' Stone returned. 'I don't get it. When you made that film everyone raved about it. You were the hottest thing since chicken vindaloo. What made you give it all up—for this?'

Leo gave him a level look. 'It's a long story, Stone,' she said dryly. 'And one I only tell to "particularly close friends".'

Marriot looked at Stone and winced. 'Ouch!' he said softly.

Stone said nothing, but for the first time there was the

beginning of a smile in his eyes.

'Anyway,' Leo continued, 'as far as Guy Farnaby is concerned Leonora Carr fits the bill very nicely. I'm decorative but undemanding and I have the right sort of background for his dilettante image. I've let him think that I got hooked on drugs while I was in Hollywood and I've never managed to kick the habit. I think he's taken the bait. He's throwing a party down at his place in Hampshire this weekend and I'm invited. We know he's expecting a consignment of drugs soon. All we need to know now is exactly when, and where. This party seems like a good place to start finding out.'

'Where do we come in?' asked Stone.

'Not at all, if I can help it,' was the terse reply. 'If Farnaby suspects that either of us is being followed we might as well pack up and go home. But I suppose there is something to be said for one of you being handy in case I need help in a hurry. Just stay out of sight, for God's sake.' She looked at her watch. 'I've got to get ready. I'm meeting him for dinner and then we're going to the opera. Help yourselves to another drink. I shan't be long.'

When the door had closed behind her both men stood silent, gazing after her. Nick Marriot drew a long breath.

'I think I'm in love!'

Stone laughed briefly. 'Forget it, sunshine. You haven't got a hope.' He yawned. 'Oh well. Looks like a shift job.'

Marriot produced a coin. 'Loser takes the first watch.'

He tossed the coin. 'Heads!' said Stone. Nick grinned. 'Hey, you're in luck!'

'You mean I get the evening off?'

'No, you get to go to the opera!'

* * *

When Leo returned they were both expecting some sort of transformation but even so the effect left them breathless for a moment. The rather unruly curls had disappeared under a wig of the same colour but dressed in an elaborate and sophisticated style. Much heavier but very skilfully applied make-up had moulded the structure of the face and made the eyes appear more enormous than ever. She was wearing a dress of jade-green chiffon and from her ears hung long jade drops set in gold. She looked, in fact, every man's ideal of the sophisticated, glamorous and totally desirable woman.

The effect she had made was not lost on Leo and when she spoke there was a hint of mockery in her tone.

'I take it you're not both "minding" me all evening?'

Marriot looked at Stone and saw him swallow.

'No. That's my—privilege—tonight.'

'Right. We're dining at Franco's in Jermyn Street—' her eyes teased him—'in case you lose me on the way. Is there any sign of my taxi out there? I ordered one.'

Nick looked out of the window. 'Not yet.'

Stone said. 'Look, if you do need me how are you going to get in touch? Do you carry one of these?' He produced his personal radio.

Leo grinned, lifted her arms and looked down at herself. A very small purse hung on her wrist.

'Where do you suggest I put it?'

'Don't answer that!' muttered Nick.

'You ought to have one,' Stone said obstinately.

'Oh, I've got one all right,' Leo told him. 'I carry one in the car and there's one in my desk—but I dare not carry anything that might connect me with Triple S when I'm using this cover.'

'How will you get hold of me if you need me, then?' Stone persisted.

'I'll either get to a phone and get Control to patch me through to your radio, or I'll give you a visual signal or send someone with a message. I know it's not ideal but it's the best I can think of.'

'Here's the taxi,' said Nick.

'Good.' Leo's tone was brisk. 'On your bike, you two. I don't want to be seen leaving with you.'

'One thing,' Stone said, turning at the door. 'If we do need to contact you at any time we shall need to know code names. I'm Delta One, he's Delta Two. What's your call sign?'

Leo smiled at him. 'I'm Omega—because...'

'Because...' they finished the sentence for her in unison, 'because you always like to have the last word!'

Chapter 5

Stone did not enjoy his evening. To start with he sat in his car parked in a side-street opposite the restaurant and munched a hamburger while Leo and Farnaby, who had a table either by accident or Leo's design right by the lighted window, ate oysters and drank champagne. Even that seemed an affront to Stone in his current mood. He was convinced that nobody consumed oysters and champagne because they actually liked them. It was simply a way of advertising superfluous wealth.

Then came the opera. Stone had never been inside Covent Garden before and for a while the place itself and its atmosphere kept him interested. His warrant card and a quiet word with the house manager earned him a seat at the side of the Grand Circle where by simply turning his head he could see Leo and Farnaby in the front row at the centre of the horseshoe. He had to admit that the plush and the gilt and the pink-shaded lamps along the edge of the balcony, together with the subdued murmur of a large and expectant audience, gave a sense of occasion, of participating in something outside of the ordinary run of experience; and when the orchestra struck up the first bars of the overture there was a sense of power and presence which you did not get with even the best hi-fi. When the curtain rose there was enough visual interest to occupy him for a while and some of the music was really quite stirring, especially the triumphal march where an apparently endless stream of soldiers and chariots and captured slaves processed across the stage; but the sight of a portly tenor in Egyptian dress bawling out his innermost feelings at the top of his extremely powerful voice struck him as simply ludicrous and he soon lost the thread of the story. After that he occupied himself by watching Leo. She sat absolutely still, leaning slightly forward, her eyes never leaving the stage. Next to her, Farnaby intermittently nodded his head or wagged his programme in time to the music and Stone saw that from time to time he glanced around the auditorium. Unmusical though he might be, Stone was still enough of a connoisseur of human nature to distinguish the genuine opera-lover from the fake.

In the interval he stood in the crush bar behind the Grand Circle and watched the people. They were a section of society he did not often get a chance to observe close to. The women, particularly, fascinated him—sleek, elegant, like prize racehorses, wafting around him as they passed a vapour trail of the kind of scent that at once excited and terrified him.

By half-way through the second act he had run out of things to occupy his mind and the next thing he was aware of was a painfully sharp dig in the ribs from his next-door neighbour. He straightened up in his seat and began the long and intermittently unsuccessful battle against sleep.

When the opera finished he hoped fervently that Leo would say good night to Farnaby and go home, but once again his luck was out. They went on to a night-club. Afraid that if he sat in the car he would fall asleep again he bought a cup of plastic coffee from an all-night stand and paced up and down with his coat collar turned up around his ears.

They came out sooner than he had dared to hope and he saw Leo shaking her head and smiling apologetically, and guessed that she had made some excuse. He just had time to get back to his car before a taxi drew up and Farnaby handed Leo into it. Stone was glad to see that he remained on the pavement, waving, as it drew away.

When the taxi deposited Leo at her flat Stone parked opposite and watched her go inside. A few seconds later the lights came on in the big front room. He settled deeper into his seat and wished that he had had the foresight to put a flask and a blanket in the back of the car. It was going to be a long, cold night.

Up in the flat, Leo went through to the kitchen, opened the small freezer and took out a plastic box labelled, in her own handwriting, 'boeuf bourguignon'. She opened it, placed it in the microwave oven, then ran her eye over the wine rack which stood in one corner and selected a bottle with the sloping shoulders of wine from Burgundy. She checked the label—Nuits St George—and drew the cork. Then she went through to the living-room and began to set the table.

Stone yawned and shivered, and remembered that he had only had a hamburger for his dinner. He wondered if there was any point in contacting Control and asking them to send out someone to take his place. Then his car radio bleeped. He jerked forward, his lethargy vanishing, and grabbed the microphone.

'Delta One.'

'Delta One, this is Omega.'

'Go ahead, Omega.'

A slight pause. Then, 'What's the weather like down there?'

Stone swore and looked up at the lighted windows. What was the bloody woman playing at now? He pressed the speak button on the microphone.

'Cold,' he said shortly.

Again the fractional pause.

'Well, what are you waiting for? Supper's almost ready.'

For the second time that day Stone entered the flat and warily pushed open the door to the sitting room. At one end of the room was a circular dinner-table, set with silver and sparkling crystal wineglasses. Leo looked up in the act of lighting two tall red candles and smiled at him.

'Why don't you pour the wine? The rest won't be long.'

A slow answering smile spread across Stone's face as he pushed the door to behind him.

* * *

Promptly at seven the next morning Nick Marriot parked his car behind Stone's, reached into the back for a flask of coffee and a packet of sandwiches and strolled up to the front off-side door. Stone wound down the window and smiled at him.

'Good-morning!'

Nick leaned down and peered in. He had expected to find his partner heavy-eyed, haggard and in a foul temper. Instead he looked kempt, relaxed and—yes, there was no other word for it—smug.

'I brought you some coffee,' Nick said.

'Thanks.' Stone took the flask but he seemed in no hurry to pour himself a drink.

Nick glanced up at the windows of the flat. 'Everything OK?'

'Oh yes—everything's fine.' Stone stretched and yawned.

'Well, I'll be on my way then.'

He started the engine and Nick stood back. 'Right. See you later.'

He watched the Capri turn out of the square, then looked up again at the windows of the flat—but they were not giving away any secrets. He decided that he ought to check on Leo's car. A short walk round the corner brought him to a mews with a row of lock-up garages. He had no way of telling which was Leo's but he satisfied himself that none of the locks had been tampered with and that there was no other way in. Very soon after, Leo appeared and went into one of the garages. There was a lengthy pause. Good girl, Nick thought, she's doing all the routine checks.

When the TR7 came out he followed at a discreet distance and soon realized where they were heading. By eight o'clock they were in the Spartacus Health Club. He watched Leo take the private lift up to Pascoe's apartment and toyed with the idea of following, but instinct told him that his boss would not appreciate his interference. While he stood undecided a telephone behind the reception desk buzzed and one of the receptionists, who were all Triple S operatives, called him over.

'Message for you from Omega. She says she will be here for an hour. Control suggests that you go and have a workout in the gym.'

'Thanks!' said Nick dryly, and took the lift to the gym which was reserved for Triple S agents, where one of the resident coaches, delighted to get his hands on one of his less enthusiastic pupils, put him through an exhaustive training session. He might have felt better about it if he had known that, after ten minutes with Pascoe, Leo was also undergoing a thorough work-out. No matter how unusual, or how highly thought of, Pascoe made it an unvarying rule that all Triple S operatives must maintain the highest standards of physical fitness.

Just before nine Control buzzed him with the message that Leo was about to leave. He followed her through the rush-hour traffic to Knightsbridge and watched her go into the offices of the Cavendish Agency. The debris of the Mini had been cleared away and the broken windows in the office mended, but there was still the evidence of a charred patch on the wall and a large oil-slick on the road for yesterday's incident.

Nick waited a few minutes, then reached into the back of the car and dragged out a donkey jacket and a wooden tool-box.

'Morning,' he said to the blonde in the office. 'Come to check your phones. We had a report that people have had difficulty getting through.'

'Well, they wouldn't, would they?' she said.

'We've only just arrived.'

'Ah, number unobtainable,' said Nick, 'not just no reply. Better check, hadn't I?'

'I suppose you had,' she agreed.

He busied himself with the phones. 'Gather you had a bit of trouble yesterday…'

'Oh don't!' the girl murmured. 'I can't bear to think about it. That poor kid!'

'Yeah, awful,' Nick agreed sympathetically.

'Mind you,' she went on, 'Miss Cavendish was marvellous. That's our boss. She was down there with a fire extinguisher while the rest of us were still screaming.

'Oh yeah?' said Nick.

The door of the inner office opened.

'What's going on in here?' Irene inquired.

'Man come to check the phones,' said the blonde.

'Has he shown you his identity card?' called Leo from inside.

'Oh, I forgot to ask!' the girl exclaimed.

Leo appeared in the doorway. 'May I?' she said, extending a hand towards him.

Nick grinned and reached into the pocket of the donkey jacket. 'Certainly, madam.'

She studied briefly the plastic-covered card which he handed her, and returned it, without a flicker of recognition.

'You'd better check the phones in my office while you're about it.'

He examined the phones while she checked the deployment of the Cavendish Agency's workers with Irene. Listening with half an ear he realized that the fact that the agency operated as a profitable business as well as simply a Triple S cover was very largely due to the efficiency of its proprietress. After ten minutes he declared that the fault must be further down the line and took his departure, satisfied that at least the phones were not being bugged and that all the Cavendish employees appeared genuine—more important, the place 'smelt' right. Nick Marriot was a great believer in gut reactions.

He expected a quiet, even tedious day. In fact, he scarcely had time to open the newspaper he had brought with him. After less than an hour in the office Leo reappeared and jumped into her car. First stop was the nearest general hospital. It was not hard to guess why and a few discreet enquiries, in the guise of a reporter, gave Nick the information that the girl, Jenny, was out of intensive care and 'as well as could be expected'. The rest of the morning was occupied in calling on prospective clients. Around twelve thirty he began to hope that Leo was about ready to stop for lunch, but not a bit of it. The TR7 drew up outside the studios of the London Contemporary Dance Theatre and Leo leapt out, carrying her ubiquitous holdall. After a while Nick drifted into the foyer. In his jeans and long hair he looked very much in keeping with the rest of the young men and women who were standing around. He peered through the glass panel in one of the doors. A dance class was in progress and in the front row was Leo, in blue tights and leotard. Nick had mixed in that world once and knew a bit about contemporary dance—enough to see that she was good, very good. But then, why not? A leading stage actress before she went to Hollywood, this would all have been part of her training. Why? Why had she given all that up to join Triple S?

After the class she came out, flushed-faced and tousle-haired, with a group of others and they headed down the street to a health food restaurant. Nick contemplated following her in, but decided in favour of a pint and a pie in the pub opposite. He had hardly had time to down the former before she was on her way again, this time to the hairdresser's. While he was waiting for her to come out Stone buzzed him on the radio and a few minutes later the bronze Capri drew up behind him.

'I don't know how she keeps it up,' Nick said. 'She hasn't

stopped all day.'

Stone grinned. 'She doesn't let up much at night, either—I mean, it was midnight before she went home last night.'

Nick looked at him narrowly but his face was blank and innocent.

'Feel like giving me a spell for an hour or two?' Nick suggested.

'Sure,' Stone agreed. 'I'll do better than that. I'll take over the night shift for you. I'm not doing anything special this evening.'

'No, no,' Nick said quickly, 'I wouldn't dream of it. You carry on for now. I'll be back to take the night shift.'

* * *

At seven that evening he parked opposite Leo's flat. Stone was sitting in his car.

'Had a quiet afternoon?' Nick asked.

'You've got to be joking,' his partner replied. 'We've been half-way down the M4 this afternoon to call on some old biddy—all in the line of business, as far as I can make out.'

Nick looked up at the windows speculatively. 'I wonder if she's going anywhere tonight.'

Stone grinned. 'I hope she takes you to a lecture on insect life in Outer Mongolia.'

'If she does, I shall send for you,' Nick returned. 'I'd hate you to miss something as fascinating as that.'

'Sure you don't want me to do this shift?' Stone asked.

'Quite sure!' Nick replied.

He watched Stone drive away and then got back into his own car. Twenty minutes passed. He began to wonder why he had been so quick to refuse Stone's offer. Then his radio bleeped.

'Delta Two.'

'Delta Two, this is Omega.'

'Go ahead, Omega.'

'Delta Two, have you had dinner?'

Nick looked up at the windows of the flat and began to smile. He could just make out a figure behind the glass.

'Not exactly. I've got some sandwiches.'

'I see. I was thinking more in terms of fresh salmon and a bottle of Chablis.'

'Sounds great!'

'Well, if you come up straight away we'll have time for a Martini before we eat.'

A few moments later Nick opened the door of the sitting-room. Leo, dressed in a loose green kaftan, was lighting tall white candles on the dinner-table.

Chapter 6

Swancombe House had been built shortly before the First World War. The Farnabys had made their money in shipping in Southampton. It was large, rambling, rather pretentious and set in a couple of acres of grounds which sloped gently down to the River Hamble. Leo stood by the windows leading out onto the terrace and looked across the dark lawns. It was easy to imagine the doomed youth of 1914 playing tennis and taking tea on those apparently endless golden afternoons; or the bright young things of the twenties driving down from London for weekend house-parties. Any of that would have seemed more fitting than what was going on behind her. She turned and looked back into the room. It was in darkness except for the pulsating disco lights and the noise level produced the same physical sensation as being beaten over the head with a steam-hammer. Leo began to edge her way through the writhing, jerking bodies towards the opposite door. Faces advanced towards her and receded again, expressionless, many of them dead white except for the dark gashes of eyes and lips, wild-haired, open-mouthed. It occurred to her that if Dante had witnessed the scene he would have come to the conclusion that Virgil had spared him the sight of the worst torments of the damned until that moment. Yet she knew, too, how easily, in another place and another mood, she could have given herself up to the ancient, ritualistic power of rhythmic movement.

She gained the far door and went out into the hall. Here, with the door closed behind her, it was possible to think again. She looked around. On the stairs four or five couples were exchanging languid kisses or simply gazing silently into space. From their wide, vague eyes Leo guessed that they were spaced out on something; but where were they getting it from? She had seen plenty of evidence so far of drugs being used but nothing actually changing hands. To her right, through an open door leading to the conservatory, she could hear the voice of the girl croupier who had been imported from London intoning her endless 'rien ne va plus'. Motto for the evening, Leo thought. Nothing's going for me, either.

Opposite her another door led to the library. This one was closed but from behind it she could hear a murmur of sound. She moved across towards it but as she reached it a large man in a dinner suit which had definitely seen better days lounged out of a chair nearby and casually interposed himself between it and her.

She gave him a steady look. 'What's the matter? Afraid I might see something I haven't seen before?'

He shrugged and moved aside. 'Up to you, miss. Just don't want anyone upset, that's all.'

Leo went inside. Her guess had been more accurate than her bluff to the man at the door. Up on the screen at the far end of the room people were doing things she had not seen before and did not want to see again. She stayed long enough to register who was in the room and then slipped out again.

'Too strong for you?' the doorman leered.

She lifted her shoulders. 'I wish they wouldn't keep rerunning these old movies.'

She went over and stood watching the roulette from the doorway of the conservatory. There was no sign of Farnaby. He had been attentive to her for the first half-hour or so of the party and had then left her with a group of his 'artistic' friends, including the boy from the *corps de ballet,* and disappeared. She reflected that, if she had not come as his guest, it would have been useful to have a partner—Stone, perhaps, or Nick Marriot. He would probably have been more at home here. On the other hand, perhaps not. The room where the music was might be filled with the trendy young, but out here the dinner suits, except for the bouncer by the library door, were hand-made in Savile Row and the diamonds were genuine—well, most of them. She had already compiled in her head an extensive and quite surprising guest list.

In the dining-room there was nothing but the remains of the excellent buffet supper and two young men who seemed to have arrived with the express purpose of getting as drunk as possible and succeeded even beyond their own expectations. Leo wondered if she should investigate the kitchen regions, or possibly upstairs. She had seen couples drifting in that direction from time to time but had assumed that she knew for what purpose, and the idea of lurking outside bedroom doors did not appeal to her. Nevertheless, it was clear that Guy Farnaby was not in any of the public rooms. She decided to try upstairs and picked her way over the supine bodies to the galleried landing above. Just as she reached it she heard Farnaby's voice from the passageway below her. He spoke quietly, but with a harsh edge which she had only heard hints of before.

'Nothing is for nothing, little girl. Just remember that. Let me know when you've thought it over.'

Then a girl's voice, very young, very desperate.

'But you can't do this to me! Guy, you've got to help me. Please, Guy!'

'Shut up!' he hissed. 'Do you want everyone to know? I've told you what to do. When you've made up your mind to co-operate you'll get what you want. Now leave me alone.'

Leo saw him cross the hall and go into the conservatory. A few seconds later a girl appeared and came blundering up the stairs, tripping over the legs of the lounging couples who stared up at her with blank indifference. As she passed Leo saw that she was a pale, painfully thin child with mousy hair frizzed out in an attempt to emulate current fashion, and a bone structure which seemed all nose and collar-bones. Something at the back of Leo's mind queried—anorexia? The girl had her hand pressed across her mouth as if she was about to be sick and seemed unaware of Leo as she rushed past. Leo watched her go down the passage and saw the door of one of the bedrooms close behind her.

A gentle tap on the door produced no response so Leo opened it and went in. A bathroom led off to one side and through the open door of this she could see the girl leaning against the wall, her arms clutched about her fragile body, shivering convulsively. Leo went across to her and took her gently by the shoulders. The girl showed no surprise but stared up at her with the huge, supplicating eyes of a wounded animal. Leo led her over to the bed and wrapped a blanket round her and then crouched in front of her, one hand clasping hers, which was icy to the touch, the other gently stroking back the dishevelled hair from the burning forehead.

'Listen,' Leo said. 'I know what you're going through, and I know why. It's bad, but I can help you. You must believe that. No matter how terrible it all seems now, I can help you if you trust me. Will you trust me?'

The girl stared down at her in silence.

'My name is Leonora,' she went on. 'What's yours?'

A long silence, as if she had forgotten—or forgotten how to speak. Then, in a husky whisper, 'Mandy. Amanda Clifton.'

'Mandy,' Leo repeated. 'OK, Mandy. If I'm going to help you I need to know the whole story.'

The girl shook her head violently. 'I can't tell you. I can't tell anybody!'

Leo took her by the shoulders. 'Yes, you can! You can, and you must, because you can't handle this by yourself any more. You need help. I can help you, but only if you tell me everything. You're on drugs, right?'

The girl dropped her head and nodded faintly.

'Heroin?' Leo persisted.

Again the faint nod.

'And Guy Farnaby gave it to you. Right?'

Once again the girl's eyes were fixed on her with that terrified animal stare.

'Look,' Leo said, 'I know all about Farnaby. You're not giving anything away. It was him, wasn't it?'

Again the girl nodded and whispered, 'Yes.'

'But now he won't give you any more?' Leo probed. 'You're suffering from withdrawal symptoms. Why has he stopped your supply?'

The girl twisted restlessly, trying to get out of Leo's grip, her tongue passing feverishly over her lips. Leo held her firmly.

'Why, Mandy?'

The girl took a deep, shuddering breath. 'Because he's trying to blackmail my father.'

'Blackmail him how?'

Mandy appeared to come to some decision and take a grip on herself. Her voice grew stronger.

'My father is the chief constable. Yesterday, Guy wrote to him and told him about me—anonymously, of course—and threatened to tell the newspapers if my father didn't do what he wanted. Daddy got the letter this morning. He made me tell him the whole story—except Guy's name. I pretended I didn't know who he was—said I used to meet him in pubs and cafes and places. I was terrified if I told him that I wouldn't get any more stuff. He's been keeping me short for days now, so I knew how awful it would be. My father said he wasn't going to give in to blackmail and he was planning to send me away to some clinic or something. He locked me in my room, but I got out and came here to see Guy, to beg him to give me a fix. He says he won't give me any more until my father agrees to do as he says.'

'But if your father is determined not to give in to blackmail...' Leo began.

The girl shook her head despairingly. 'He'll have to give in in the end. You see, Guy didn't tell him everything. If he goes to the police, I shall go to prison!'

'Mandy,' Leo said gently, 'they don't send people to prison just for using heroin.'

'No,' she said bitterly, 'but they do for bringing it into the country.'

'You carried H through customs for Farnaby?'

'Yes.' The girl sighed despairingly. 'I started using it about a year ago. He made it easy for me at first. Then, when I was hooked, the price started going up. When I told him I couldn't afford it he suggested I could make some extra money when we went away on our summer holidays. We have a villa in Greece, you see, where we go every year. He arranged it all. He told me to buy a doll in traditional costume—you know the sort of thing. Someone must have swapped it for another one, I don't know when. When I got back I took it to Guy and he showed me the hollowed-out place in the centre where the heroin was. So you see...'

She broke off, shaking her head and beginning to shiver again. Leo said urgently,

'You were forced into it, Mandy. No jury would really blame you. If you help me to catch Farnaby and get him put away I'm sure you will be all right.'

Mandy looked at her. 'Are you a policewoman?'

'Not exactly, but I work with the police,' Leo told her. 'We want to stop Farnaby before he hurts even more people like you. Now tell me what was it that he wanted your father to do?'

'Do?' the girl repeated vaguely.

'He threatened to tell the papers about you if your father didn't do what he wanted. What was it?'

'He said something about "your men have been snooping around boat-houses on the river. Tell them to keep away".'

'Just 'boat-houses'? He didn't say anything more specific?'

'No. But Guy has a boat-house.'

'Here?'

'No. On the opposite side. I saw him there one day when I was sailing with a friend. There's a big old house that's used as an old people's home or something. The boat-house is in the grounds. I suppose he rents it or something.'

Leo took the girl's hands in both her own and squeezed them. 'Good girl! That's just the sort of information I needed. Now listen. Are you staying here for the night?'

'I suppose so.' Mandy shrugged and choked back a sob. 'There's nowhere else to go. Guy always lets me stay when I come to parties.'

'Right,' Leo said. 'This is what you must do. Now listen, Mandy. You must do exactly what I tell you if I'm going to help you, no matter how bad you're feeling. Do you promise?'

The girl nodded bleakly.

'I'm going to leave you here for a little while because we can't get out of the house without being seen until the party is over. When I go I'm going to lock the door, not to keep you in but to make sure nobody comes bothering you.'

'Why can't I lock it?' Mandy asked.

'Because you might fall asleep and I don't want to have to rouse half the house trying to wake you when I come back. I've got some friends near here. I'm going to contact them and ask them to bring a car. Then, when everyone is asleep, I shall come and fetch you and take you to them. They will see that you get to a place where you'll be looked after and helped to kick your habit. That is what you want, isn't it?'

'I suppose so,' Mandy muttered uncertainly. 'What about my parents?'

'I'll see that they are informed of where you are. I should think they'll be able to come and visit you tomorrow. Now, you lie down and try to get some sleep. I'll be back in an hour or so, when things have quietened down.'

Leo settled the waif-like little figure on the bed and tucked the blankets around her.

'Now try not to worry. Just lie quiet. Everything's going to be all right.'

She moved softly to the door and slipped out into the passage. There was nobody in sight. She locked the door, praying that Mandy would not panic and start hammering to be let out, and went swiftly to her own room. There she unearthed the radio transceiver which, after some heart-searching, she had agreed to include in her luggage, and switched it on.

'Delta One, this is Omega. Come in please.'

There was a brief silence. Then to her relief she heard Nick's voice.

'Delta Two, actually. The watch has changed. And yes, I have had supper, but I can always eat another one.'

In spite of her tension Leo found herself smiling.

'Stop fooling, Delta Two. This is business. I shall have a passenger for you in an hour or two. Where shall I find you?'

'You've seen the stretch of woodland opposite the main gate? About two hundred yards east of the gate there's a bridle-path. I'm twenty or thirty yards in off the road.'

'Is Delta One with you?'

'No, but I can raise him.'

'Do that. I shall want both of you. I can't tell exactly when. Just be there. Omega out.'

Leo hid the radio again amongst her clothing and went back to the party, which showed no signs as yet of breaking up.

* * *

Stone's car nosed its way up the dark bridle-path and came to rest beside Marriot's. He got out and slid into the passenger seat beside Nick.

'What's going on?'

'Nothing so far,' Nick told him. 'Just a message from Leo telling us to stand by and saying she'd be bringing us a "passenger".'

'You don't suppose she's decided to pick up Farnaby, all off her own bat, do you?' Stone asked.

'Wouldn't put it past her,' Nick said with a grin, 'but what would be the point?'

'Oh well, we'll just have to wait and see, I suppose,' Stone yawned. 'But it had better be good. I was on my way to bed.'

'With or without that blonde barmaid?' Nick asked.

'What barmaid?' Stone countered innocently.

Half an hour or more passed before they heard a car approach, slow down to turn out of the drive and then accelerate to pass the end of the track. It was followed by another, then a whole convoy, their lights briefly illuminating the trees as they hummed away into the darkness.

'Party's breaking up at last,' Stone commented.

'Yeah. Fancy getting in among that lot with a breathalyser!' Nick grinned.

'You know your trouble,' Stone told him. 'You think like a policeman.'

A long silence followed the passing of the last car. Nick stretched.

'She'd better make it soon. It'll be dawn before long.'

He got out of the car and moved a few paces towards the road. The May night was mild, with a milky sky that had never become really dark. Apart from the faint, constant hushing of the wind in the leaves overhead the silence was complete. Then he heard the sound of footsteps and a faint murmur of voices and a second later Leo appeared, silhouetted for a moment against the paler surface of the roadway, clutching another huddled shape which she appeared to be half carrying. Nick went forward quickly and helped to support the shuddering, sobbing girl back to where the cars were parked. Stone got out and came to meet them.

'Who is she, Leo?'

'Her name is Amanda Clifton. Her father is the chief constable.' Leo turned Mandy towards her and looked into her face. 'Mandy, these are friends of mine. This is Stone, and this one is Nick Marriot. He'll look after you and take you to somewhere safe.'

The girl stared helplessly at Nick and caught her breath on a strangled sob. He reached out and took her in his arms, holding her head against his shoulder, where she nestled as if she had found a refuge.

'Don't worry, love,' he said gently. 'I'll see you're all right.' Then, looking over her head at Leo, 'Some of Farnaby's handiwork?'

Leo nodded. 'I'm afraid so. Now he's trying to blackmail the father. Nick, she needs to be taken somewhere where they have experience of this kind of thing, but somewhere where she'll be safe and where they can keep their mouths shut.'

'Don't worry,' Nick told her. 'I know just the place. It's a private clinic in Surrey. They know me there. I'll take her straight away.'

'Good,' Leo's voice expressed considerable relief. 'Can you contact her parents when you've got her settled? She's run away, so they're probably going spare.'

'Will do,' Nick agreed. 'What then? Do you want me back here?'

'Yes,' said Leo. 'I think the balloon's going up here fairly soon. I'll fill Stone in with all the details. You contact him as soon as you get back. Have you got a base down here?'

Stone nodded briefly. 'We're booked in at the local pub. If I'm not there when you get back, Nick, wait until you hear from me.' 'Right.' Nick turned towards his car, his arm still tight round the girl. 'Come on, Mandy. The sooner we get you to someone who can help you the better.'

Leo helped him to tuck her up on the back seat with a rug over her and she and Stone stood and watched until the rear lights disappeared on the road.

'Good old Nick,' Leo said quietly. 'He was very sweet with her.'

'Yes,' Stone agreed. Then added, 'Well, it's not the first time for him.'

Leo glanced at him. 'Meaning?'

'Meaning he's had a lot of experience with drug cases.'

'Drugs Squad?' Leo asked.

Stone turned and led the way back to his car.

'For a time. But that wasn't really what I was thinking of.' He opened the passenger door. 'Let's get in, shall we. It's warmer.'

They settled themselves in the car. Leo said, 'What were you thinking of—about Nick, I mean?'

Stone hesitated. Reticence about personal matters, his own and other people's, was part of his nature. Yet there was something about the pre-dawn stillness and Leo's closeness in the seat beside him which weakened his defences.

'He was involved in that scene himself for a while. I don't mean he used dope, at least nothing stronger than the occasional whiff of pot, but he had a girl-friend who was hooked on heroin.'

'How did he get into that scene?' Leo asked.

'When he left school he wanted to get into the pop music world. It was the mid seventies when "dropping out" was still fashionable, if you remember, and it was all pot and protest songs—a hangover from the hippies and all that. Nick plays guitar and writes his own songs…

'Still?' Leo asked.

'Well, sometimes. Catch him in the right mood and he'll give you a sample. In those days he was convinced he could make a living at it. Nearly broke his parents' hearts, I gather. He comes from a very respectable family—father's a doctor somewhere in Warwickshire. Minor public school, all that—they were expecting to turn out a lawyer or another medic or something. Instead, they found they'd got a rebel on their hands. Anyway, he struggled on for a couple of years, just about keeping his head above water. To do him justice, he never asked his parents for a penny—his mother told me that, he didn't. Then he met this girl—Jacky. She was doing the same kind of thing, but she was deeply into drugs before he ever met her. He tried for six months to help her kick the habit, then somebody sold her some bad dope and it killed her. It really broke Nick up. He went on a kind of one-man crusade against the pushers who had been responsible. Of course, it wasn't long before he came up against the law. For a bit he wasn't really sure whether they were on his side or against him.' Stone grinned briefly. 'I think he still has the same problem from time to time. Then he met up with a young det. sergeant who persuaded him that if he wanted to get back at the big guys who were really responsible the only way to do it was to join the police. So he did.'

'That must have come as a bit of a shock, after the life he'd been leading,' Leo commented.

'I'm not sure who got the biggest shock, him or the police force,' Stone agreed with a chuckle. 'Anyhow, he survived his training somehow and eventually got transferred to the Drugs Squad, where he went through the London drug scene like the wrath of God. The trouble was, he was so successful that he outlived his usefulness—made himself too well known. His superiors couldn't persuade him to keep a low profile and they were afraid they were going to have a fatality on their hands. Somebody brought him to Pascoe's attention and he was recruited into Triple S.'

'Bit of a contrast with the pot and flower-power scene,' Leo said.

'Not as much as you might think,' Stone said quietly. 'Nick's an idealist, you see. Once he'd have been a crusader or a knight errant or something. Now…'

'Now it's Triple S?' Leo laughed softly. 'Is that how you see it, Stone—the modern equivalent of the Knights of Malta?'

'Oh no,' he laughed too, shaking his head. 'I'm talking about Nick, not me.'

'Speaking with the authority of one who knows, though,' Leo commented.

Stone shrugged and was silent for a moment. 'You work with a man in this sort of job for getting on for three years,' he said at length, 'you get to know what makes him tick.'

'Obviously,' she agreed. 'Although I should have said it was a case of chalk and cheese.'

'Oh?' he looked at her, smiling.

'Well, I should imagine they breed a pretty gritty type of

realist around the Liverpool area.'

'Have you seen my file?' he asked sharply.

'Oh, now, how could I?' she murmured. 'You know personal files are sacred.'

'Then how do you know I come from that area?'

'It's in your voice.'

She saw his face tighten and began to understand that she must tread carefully.

'I didn't realize it was that obvious.'

'It's not. I doubt if most people would notice anything. But you've got to remember that voices and accents are part of my stock in trade.'

He relaxed slightly. 'Yes, of course. But you're not quite spot on, anyway—the other side of the Mersey, Birkenhead.'

'So—' she leaned back in her seat and looked at him—'how does a tough lad from Birkenhead come to be playing cops and robbers with a knight in shining armour from Warwickshire?'

'Via the RAF, among other things—but that's a long story—and one...'

'And one you only tell to particularly close friends,' she finished for him, and they both laughed.

He stretched his arm along the back of her seat.

'Do you think we've reached a sufficiently advanced stage of intimacy for that?'

'Well, now,' she murmured, 'what happened the other night is one thing, but swapping life stories...' Her eyes teased him. He leaned towards her.

'Well, perhaps we should double-check, before we say anything we might regret.'

She put her fingers on his lips.

'Not during working hours. It's strictly against my principles.'

'It's strictly against my principles to work at three o'clock in the morning,' he grunted. 'However, if you insist...'

'I don't know why I'm sitting here gossiping with you anyway,' she said, 'except that it's nice to talk to someone relatively normal for a few minutes. But I've got to get back before light, so listen. I think I know where Farnaby is landing the dope.'

'How did you find that out?' he asked, his amorous intentions receding to the back of his mind.

'That girl—Mandy. You remember I said her father is the chief constable? Farnaby is trying to blackmail him. Apparently the local police have been keeping an eye on the boathouses along the river. Farnaby wants Clifton to warn them off. And Mandy says she has seen him at a boat-house on the opposite side of the river. It belongs to a big house which is now an old people's home, so it shouldn't be too hard to identify. We know Farnaby's expecting a consignment soon and the fact that he's decided this is the moment to use his hold over Clifton confirms that. My bet is that it'll be sometime in the next couple of nights.'

'Sounds probable,' Stone agreed. 'So what do you want me to do?'

'Get onto Pascoe for a start. Tell him the story and get him to talk to Clifton. Tell him to call his men off, as if he's giving in to Farnaby. Then you and Nick identify the boat-house and keep an eye on it. I'm going to find an excuse for staying on when the rest of the house-party leave tomorrow. As soon as I get any hint of something going on I'll call you.'

'Leo—' he turned to her seriously—'take care, for God's sake. If Farnaby is expecting a delivery he's not going to want anyone hanging around. If he gets the idea that you're spying on him he could turn very nasty. Why don't you go back to London with the others and leave me and Nick to sort things out here? After all, it's only a matter of keeping the boat-house under surveillance and then calling in the local boys as soon as something happens.'

'By the time you're sure something is going on and the local force have got to you it could be all over,' Leo pointed out. 'What you need is advanced warning, and that's what I'm going to try to give you.' She opened the car door. 'I've got to get back. I'll be in touch, either later today or tomorrow.'

He walked to the end of the track with her.

'Are you sure you can get in again? Nick and I had a look round the perimeter and it looked pretty secure.

'Yes, his system's not bad,' Leo agreed, 'but after a party like that it isn't surprising that someone, somewhere, forgot to check all the switches—is it? Don't worry. I'll get back all right. Incidentally—'she paused and looked at him quizzically—'what does mine host at the pub think you two are up to, going in and out at all hours?'

'He thinks we're a couple of ardent ornithologists, looking for nightingales,' Stone told her.

Leo grinned. 'Some bird-watchers!'

He grinned back. 'Some bird!'

Chapter 7

Very few of the guests at Swancombe put in an appearance before mid-morning and it was after lunch before most of them were ready to set off back to Town, so it caused no particular comment when Leonora, who had been seen dancing wildly during the last hour or so of the party, came down at midday looking pale and distinctly hung over. She toyed with a little iced consommé at lunch and then murmured something about lying down and retired to her room again. It was not until after the last of his guests had finally departed that Farnaby realized he had not seen her since then and went in search of her. He found her in her room, lying on the bed dressed only in a black silk slip. She was completely unconscious and on the bedside table lay a hypodermic syringe and an empty ampoule.

Farnaby bent over her and pulled back her eyelids, then felt her pulse. He picked up the syringe and examined it and stood for a long moment in thought. Then he went out, locking the door behind him and made his way down to the library where Stringer, his chauffeur— the man who had been standing guard at the library door the previous evening—was waiting for him.

'Silly bitch has shot herself so full of something she's dead to the world up there.'

'Difficult,' commented Stringer.

'Yes,' agreed Farnaby, 'but perhaps useful as well. We may have found ourselves another satisfied customer, Stringer.'

'What are you going to do with her?' Stringer asked.

'Leave her for the time being. She obviously isn't going to come round for an hour or so. After that—well, we can't shove her into her motor, point her in the direction of London and tell her to push off. She probably wouldn't get more than a couple of miles before she crashed, or got picked up by the police. And that could lead to some very awkward questions. No, we offer her our hospitality for the night, and then we give her a little nightcap—just to make sure she has a good night's sleep. She won't give us any bother.'

* * *

Leo heaved a deep sigh and hauled herself out of the deep, glutinous waters in which she had been floating in her dream. Her mouth tasted like an old sock and she had trouble focusing her eyes. She turned her head and winced at the sight of the syringe. It had taken more courage than many, much more dangerous activities to stick that needle in herself. Davies, the Triple S medic, had better be right about the stuffs being harmless and non-addictive, she reflected. It had needed a good deal of persuasion to get it out of him at all; but she had finally convinced him that, for her own safety, it might be necessary for her to 'do a Juliet'.

She lay for a while, listening for noises in the house. The late afternoon sun was slanting through her windows. It had been a gamble, rendering herself unconscious for such a long part of the afternoon, but she had assumed that if Farnaby was expecting anything it would not happen until after dark. The important thing was to remain in the house until then. It took some time for her head to clear so it was no hardship to stay where she was until she heard footsteps approaching her door and the small click of the key turning in the lock. She chalked up a mental plus point—Farnaby had been in to check on her, so it was as well that she had actually used the drug instead of just faking it.

As he came over to the bed she rolled lazily onto her back and smiled up at him.

'Well, well.' Farnaby sat on the edge of the bed and took one of her hands in both his own. 'Who's a silly girl then?'

'Oh Guy,' she murmured, 'I don't think either of us should be calling each other names, after what was going on last night, do you?'

He chuckled. 'Of course not. After all, we're both broadminded, aren't we?'

She raised herself on one elbow and spoke with more intensity. 'Listen, can you get the stuff for me? The bloke I've been dealing with is mucking me about. Besides, I think he's cutting it with something nasty. I need to find a new source of supply.'

He patted her hand. 'I'll have to see what I can do for you, shan't I? I might just know somebody who knows somebody—you know how it is…'

She lay back and smiled at him. 'Oh yes, I know how it is. Dear Guy, thank you so much. And if I can ever do anything for you…'

'I'm sure I'll think of something,' he purred. 'But right now I want you to stay here and rest. We can't have you going back to Town tonight, can we? I'll get Mrs Bradley to bring you up a nice little supper on a tray, and then you can have a good sleep. Right?'

She nestled a little deeper into the pillows. 'You're so sweet to me, darling. That would be lovely.'

He left her and she heard that he did not lock the door. 'Clever of him', she thought. 'I might just have decided to get up and he would have been hard put to it to find an excuse for locking me in.' Half an hour later the housekeeper appeared with a beautifully arranged tray on which were an omelette, some salad, a chocolate mousse and a pot of tea. Leo looked at it longingly. She had not eaten since the previous evening and, with her mouth still tasting as it did, the tea was particularly appealing. However, she contented herself with a long drink of water from the tap in her bathroom and then took her suitcase from the wardrobe. Tucked into one of the pockets was a chocolate bar and a packet of nuts and raisins. When she had eaten them the food on the tray still looked attractive, but resistible. She disposed of it without trouble down the lavatory, being careful to leave a few dregs of tea in the cup and even pressing her mouth to it so that it was faintly smeared with lipstick. Then she got right into the bed and settled down to wait.

The sunlight faded and the sky outside her window took on a deeper tone. The room itself grew shadowy. At length she heard the soft footsteps returning. She turned on her side and drew the sheet up so that it almost covered her face. It took a great deal of self-control to remain still while whoever it was crossed the room and stood looking down at her. She breathed deeply, simulating sleep. A hand stirred the sheet, lifting it away from her face. Then it was dropped again and the footsteps receded, followed by the closing of the door and the faint click of the lock. Even then Leo did not move until she heard Farnaby speaking to someone on the stairs.

A few minutes later she heard a car on the gravel drive. She got up quickly and went to the window, which looked out onto the front of the house. Standing to one side, where she could see without risk of being seen, she saw the car waiting outside the front door with its engine running. It was not Farnaby's familiar Rolls Royce, but an anonymous dark blue Cortina. As she watched, Farnaby came out of the house dressed in oilskins and Wellington boots. Fie was followed by his manservant, Cole, carrying a fishing-rod and a tackle box. Leo grinned to herself as she thought of Stone and Marriot earnestly listening for nightingales while Farnaby 'fished'.

As soon as the car had driven away Leo went to the drawer and took out her radio.

'Delta One and Two, this is Omega. Come in please.'

Apart from the faint hiss and crackle, silence.

'Delta One, are you receiving me? Come in please.'

Another silence, then Nick's voice, slightly breathless. 'Omega, this is Delta Two.'

'What sort of bird have you been watching?' Leo asked drily. 'Never mind, don't answer that. There's a game bird heading in your direction in a dark blue Cortina, registration number PYG 323T. If you can put him in the bag a lot of people might be having cold turkey for supper.'

'Roger, Omega.' Nick's voice was cool and efficient. 'We'll be waiting for him. What about you?'

'I'm coming to join you. Don't start without me! Omega out.'

Leo replaced the radio and dressed rapidly in dark trousers and jersey. Then she got out her suitcase again, removed the hairdryer and the pair of shoes which she had left in it and lifted out the false bottom. Fitted snugly into a specially moulded section was a Walther PPK with a shoulder holster. Leo paused, looking at it. She could think of at least four good reasons for not carrying it. On the other hand she had a feeling that tonight it might turn out to be essential. She put it on and pulled a navy anorak on over it. Then, as an afterthought, she took a spare clip and slipped it into her pocket. Next she took from the suitcase an innocent-looking piece of wire, replaced the false bottom and returned the case to the wardrobe. Finally, she pulled some spare pillows from the top shelf and made a fairly convincing humped shape under the bedclothes.

It took perhaps thirty seconds of delicate manoeuvring with the wire before the lock clicked back and she stepped out into the passage. The house was silent. She knew there were only three living-in servants at Swancombe, Cole and Stirling, the so-called chauffeur, who had both gone with Farnaby, and Mrs Bradley. Leo had no doubt that the two men were a couple of heavies recruited from the underworld to act as Farnaby's bodyguards but she was less sure about Mrs Bradley. She was inclined to believe that her worst crime was closing her eyes to the odd goings-on at Farnaby's parties. At all events, she had to hope that that was the case and the woman had not been left with orders to keep watch on her. She glided light-footed down the stairs. The hall was empty. Leo wondered if the burglar alarms had been set and turned to the passageway that led towards the kitchen area. She knew that Mrs Bradley had her own rooms somewhere in this region and the sound of a television set suggested that they were not far away. Leo opened the door of the lobby where the controls for the alarm system were situated and saw with relief that they had not yet been set. She closed the door and padded silently back to the hall. Ignoring the front door she went into the drawing-room, now restored to order after the dancing of the previous evening, and crossed to the French windows. They were locked but the key was in place. She turned it and stepped out onto the terrace.

It was full dark by now and, as none of the rooms on that side of the house were lighted, the garden lay before her in deep shadow. She crossed the lawn quickly, heading for where she knew it ended in the waters of the Hamble. A short way upstream she found what she was looking for—a dinghy with an outboard motor which she had noticed tied up to a small landing-stage the previous day. Leo climbed aboard and cast off. Ignoring the motor she took up the oars and began to pull for the opposite bank. Hidden away safely at the bottom of her suitcase back in the house was a large-scale map of the area, on which she had identified without much difficulty the old people's home where Farnaby's boathouse was. With the mental image of that clearly before her, she leaned on the oars and allowed the current to carry her downstream towards the estuary.

* * *

Stone shifted uncomfortably. Sitting on top of a wall with the branch of an oak tree digging into his shoulder-blade was not his favourite occupation.

'Sod ornithology for a living!' he muttered. 'I've had enough of this.'

In the almost total darkness among the tree branches beside him Nick Marriot chuckled softly.

'And we haven't heard so much as a chirrup from a nightingale…' He broke off. 'Hang about. Listen.'

'That was a duck, not a nightingale,' Stone told him. 'Even I know that.'

'Not birds, you fool,' Nick whispered. 'A car.'

A few seconds later they saw the headlights of the car bouncing down the rutted track which led to the boat-house.

'Heads down,' muttered Stone, and they both hid their faces from the beam until the car had passed below them and parked by the landing-stage.

The boat-house was quite large and looked as if it might once have been used for a boatbuilding business. It had clearly fallen into disrepair but an inspection during daylight had shown that recently someone had fitted new doors and window-frames and replaced rotten timbers in the landing-stage. They saw Farnaby unlock the side door and go inside, followed by the other two men.

'He's not too bothered about anyone spotting him,' Nick murmured.

'You saw the gear,' Stone replied. 'Any queries, he's having an innocent bit of night fishing.'

A long wait followed.

'I wonder where Leo is,' Nick whispered.

Stone grinned in the darkness. 'Probably floating around out there disguised as a coot or something.'

'Oh come on!' Nick protested. 'A swan, surely.'

'You've got birds on the brain.'

'I've got birds on the brain!'

'Quiet!' Stone cocked his head towards the river. Faintly, over the rustle of the wind in the trees and the lapping of the water under the landing-stage, they both heard the steady throb of a marine diesel engine. The door of the boat-house opened and Farnaby and his two men came out and stood looking down the estuary. In a few minutes they saw the masthead and port navigation lights of an approaching vessel and a sleek, ocean-going motor yacht glided almost silently up to the landing-stage. Cole and Stirling caught the mooring ropes and almost before they had fastened them three men came ashore, to be greeted by Farnaby. There was a murmured conversation and an exchange of handshakes and then Farnaby and two of the men withdrew towards the boat-house while the third helped Cole and Stirling to unload a number of packages which they transferred to the boot of the Cortina.

'That's the evidence we need,' Stone whispered.

'When do we take them?' Nick asked.

'It'll have to be soon if we want to get them all,' Stone replied. He eased his position, trying to loosen cramped muscles and at the same time freeing his gun in the shoulder holster. It had been his decision not to alert the local police for fear of frightening Farnaby off, but now he was beginning to wonder if he had been wrong. 'I wish to hell I knew what Leo's playing at,' he muttered.

The unloading was finished. Cole collected Farnaby's rod and tackle box and went on board the yacht with them.

'Clever!' whispered Nick. 'If anyone asks questions, the boat just put in here to pick him up for the fishing trip.'

'Time to move,' said Stone. 'You take the chauffeur and the two men on the yacht, and I'll deal with Farnaby and the other two.'

He twisted round and dropped silently onto the track below

the wall. Nick followed him. They drew their weapons and crept like shadows towards the landing-stage. As they approached it one of the men with Farnaby struck a match to light a cigarette and as he bent his head to the flame Stone experienced a shock of recognition—a shock which seemed to take physical form in a sudden splitting pain in the back of his skull.

For a while he was conscious of nothing except the pain and the ensuing nausea. Then he became aware that he was on the ground, that he had lost his gun and that somebody had a knee in the small of his back.

'Don't make a sound!' a voice hissed, and he felt the barrel of a pistol cold against his neck.

He heard the engine of a car start and, twisting his face out of the rough grass, saw the headlights of the Cortina sweep past him a few yards away. The knee was removed from his back.

'Get up!'

He staggered to his feet and saw that nearby Nick was being hauled to his. One man behind him, another with Nick, and a third was moving away towards the boat-house. But where had they come from—and who were they working for? He tried to turn his head to see if there were any more of them but was rewarded with a vicious jab in the spine from the barrel of his captor's pistol.

'Move! That way.'

As he walked towards the landing-stage Stone saw that the yacht had already put off and was heading downstream with Farnaby on the deck. The rest were presumably either on board or had gone in the car because only one remained. Seeing him, Stone remembered the face lit by the flare of the match. Stratos Zahran! Only six months ago his photograph had been circulated all round Triple S as a known terrorist hit-man who had entered the country illegally. One of Stone's colleagues had found him, on that occasion, and he had been deported. Now he was back—thanks to Farnaby.

The leader of the three who had ambushed them had reached Zahran and greeted him with an embrace. Then he turned and indicated Stone and Marriot. As they stumbled onto the landing-stage he was saying,

'We were waiting back there for the rest of them to get out of the way. We saw these two drop out of a tree. They were planning to take all of you.'

Zahran jerked his head. 'Bring them.' They were shoved forward. 'Search them.'

They were quickly relieved of their radios, handcuffs and warrant cards. Zahran cast his eye over them.

'SSS. Of course, it would be! You people are beginning to annoy me.' He turned to the man beside him. 'We have no time to waste on them. They cannot have known who to expect or there would have been more of them. Your men can finish them after we have gone and dump the bodies in the river. Where is your car?'

'Back there on the road.'

'Come then.' Zahran picked up a small suitcase. 'The sooner we are on the way the better.'

He began to walk away up the track. The leader of the reception committee turned to the other two.

'You heard him. Do it!'

Then he went quickly after Zahran. There was a silence, broken when the man guarding Nick spat out a word, the meaning of which was perfectly clear although the language was one which Stone could not recognize.

'Bloody marvellous!' said his companion. 'Leave us to do the dirty work!'

'Shoot them and get it over,' said the foreigner, who was dark-haired and olive-skinned.

'Oh sure!' exclaimed the other. 'And dump them in the river for the pigs to find, with slugs from our guns in them.'

'So what?' demanded the dark one.

'So it's too risky! We'll tie them up and weight them and then chuck them in. That way there'll be less chance of connecting us with the bodies.'

Stone looked around him, trying to assess the chances of jumping them before it was too late. Nick's head was drooping and he appeared to be swaying slightly. His attacker must have hit him very hard and he was clearly in no condition to make a sudden move. Stone sought desperately for a way of distracting the two men's attention long enough for him to grab the gun from the one nearest him. But even if he achieved that much he could not be sure of disabling the other one before he shot Nick.

Suddenly the dark man swung round. 'Who's there?' There might just have been a chance if Nick had been alert but before he could react his captor grabbed him by the arm and swung him across in front of him, his gun pressed into his ribs.

'What is it?' the Englishman asked tensely.

'I thought I heard something out there, on the water—oars, perhaps.'

They listened.

'Probably a water-rat or something,' said the Englishman.

Then, out of the darkness, came a woman's voice.

'Don't shoot! Where's Zahran?'

The two men exchanged rapid glances.

'Come here,' called the Englishman. 'Who are you?'

There was a splash of oars and a gentle bump and then Leo scrambled up onto the landing-stage.

'Who are you?' the man repeated.

She looked from him to his companion and then addressed the latter rapidly in his own language. He listened, nodded and appeared to relax a little.

'She says she's come from Bin Sayeed with a message for Zahran.'

'What message?'

'I cannot tell it to you,' Leo replied, her voice lightly accented. 'Only to Zahran.'

'So who are you? Where have you come from? You're not Arab—no way!'

'No, I am not. Have I said that I was? My nationality is Lebanese, but my parents were Greek. My name is Despina.'

'How did you get here? What were you doing paddling around out there?'

1 came in by air today. They sent me because I am not known in this country. I hired a car and drove down but some fool told me the wrong place for the rendezvous. I went to Farnaby's house, on the other side of the river. When there was no sign of the yacht there I stole the little boat to try and find it. I saw it

going away again, but I thought Zahran would be here.'

'He's gone,' the Englishman told her.

She spoke to the other man again in his own language and he replied. Stone thought he saw a chance and braced himself to kick out but the Arab was still on his guard. He jerked his gun towards Stone and said sharply,

'Watch him! He's going to try something.' The Englishman caught Stone with a vicious backhand swipe across the mouth and sent him staggering.

'Who are these men?' Leo inquired unemotionally.

'Government agents,' said the Englishman. 'They were waiting for the yacht. Zahran told us to finish them and drop them in the river.'

'Take them in there and tie them up,' the Arab told him. 'We'll decide how to deal with them when we've sorted this out.'

Stone had no alternative but to yield as they were pushed at gunpoint round the side of the building. The rear door had been left unlocked, either by accident or design, and within minutes both he and Marriot were fastened by their own handcuffs to a couple of stout iron stanchions at the far end, where they could no longer hear what was being said outside.

'Have you interrogated them?' Leo asked when the two men returned.

'There's no time,' the Englishman said curtly. 'And no need. We know who they are.'

'But don't you want to know why they were here?' she persisted.

'I've told you, there's no time,' he snapped. 'We should have been clear of this place long ago. Let's get back to you. You say your name is Despina and you come from Bin Sayeed. Can you prove that?'

She flashed him a look of contempt. 'Would I carry that sort of proof on me? Isn't it enough that I know Bin Sayeed, and that I knew Zahran was due here tonight? Take me to him quickly.'

The Englishman grinned suddenly. 'OK. You want us to believe you. I tell you how you can convince us. You can shoot these two— prove whose side you're on.'

The Arab made a guttural sound of protest. 'It is not a woman's job.'

'Stuff that!' his companion said sharply. 'You know as well as I do that your women are as good with a gun as most of the men. If she's been trained by Bin Sayeed she won't be afraid to pull a trigger.' He turned to Leo. 'Well?'

She shrugged indifferently. 'I'll do it—since you are afraid to do it yourselves. Bring one of them out here—the young one. He may crack and tell us something before he dies.'

'Fetch him.'

The Arab went inside.

'Do you have a gun?'

Leo took out the Walther and ejected the clip of shells.

'What are you doing?' he asked.

'Checking,' she replied calmly.

He turned as the Arab brought Nick round the corner of the building. When he looked back at Leo she was replacing the clip, and screwing on the silencer.

'Over there, in front of the doors,' the Englishman said.

Nick stood where he was put, gazing intently at Leo. He was steadier on his feet now and his eyes were clearer.

'Well, my friend,' Leo remarked, balancing the gun casually in one hand, 'are you going to tell us why you are here?'

'You're going to shoot me anyway,' he replied. 'Why should I tell you anything?'

'Get on with it and get it over,' the Englishman said restlessly.

Leo laughed. 'Look at him! What an actor he is. See how he is pretending that he does not believe I will shoot him? See how he pretends not to be afraid?'

'Will you get on with it!' The words were ground out between clenched teeth.

'Very well.' Leo raised the gun in both hands and aimed it steadily at Nick's heart. 'Let us see how good an actor you really are. How long can you go on pretending?'

Her eyes gazed into Nick's over the faint gleam of the gun barrel. He stared back as if hypnotized. Leo's finger squeezed the trigger.

The gun coughed once. Nick's body shot backwards and

thudded into the wooden doors behind him, then jack-knifed over, his hands clutching at his chest, his eyes still staring towards Leo, and finally toppled forward to lie face down on the boards of the landing-stage. It twitched once, convulsively, and was still.

Leo looked down at it expressionlessly.

'Bring the other one,' she said.

The Arab moved back towards the door. Inside they heard a sudden crash and the sound of feet kicking against the wall. Stone had heard the shot and was struggling desperately to get free.

'Go with him,' Leo said. 'That one is dangerous.'

The Englishman hesitated and she exclaimed, 'Go! You don't think I am afraid to be left alone with a body, do you?'

He turned and disappeared round the corner. As soon as he was out of sight Leo, moving with the dancer's speed and lightness of foot, went to pick up Nick's gun from where the men had dropped it when he was searched.

Then she moved over to crouch beside his body. His eyelids flickered and he looked up.

'Was I OK?'

'Brilliant, darling,' she murmured. 'Not a dry eye in the house. But we don't have time to stay for the curtain calls. Here.'

She handed him his gun. He took it and rolled on his face again, concealing it beneath his body. They could hear Stone struggling and swearing as he was dragged out of the boathouse. Leo moved away, replacing as she went the clip in her gun with one taken from her pocket. When they rounded the corner of the building with Stone she was leaning casually against a bollard.

Stone saw Nick's body as soon as he came round the corner and even in the starlight Leo saw his jaw clench and his eyes, when he looked towards her, glittered like frost. The thought crossed her mind that she would not give much for the chances of anyone who had really harmed Nick Marriot as long as Stone was alive. Aloud she said,

'Bring him here. The light's better away from the building.'

As soon as he was out of their line of sight Nick rolled over and came soundlessly to his feet, the gun in both hands.

'OK. That's far enough. Just stop right there.'

The Arab stood rigid, as if terrified to look behind him, but the other swung round, starting to lift his pistol.

'Don't do it!' Leo warned him. 'You're between the Devil and the deep blue sea.'

He stared from her to Nick and back again. 'Shit!' he said.

Stone closed his eyes for a moment and took a long breath, like a man coming up from a deep dive.

'You know, for a moment,' he said, 'you almost had me worried.'

'Had you worried!' Nick exclaimed. 'She practically scared me to death. If you hadn't given me that clue about acting, Leo, I think I'd probably have died of heart failure.'

She grinned at him. 'Never mind, love, one more performance like that and you'll be able to apply for your Equity card.' She looked at the two prisoners. 'Hadn't you better do something about them?'

Once the men had been searched and handcuffed in their turn to the stanchions in the boat-house Leo, Stone and Nick settled down on some boxes at the opposite end for a conference.

'Right,' said Stone. 'Next step... Obviously Zahran is the first priority, but do we call in the local force to search the house while we're reasonably sure the dope is still there or do we wait for Farnaby to come back from his "fishing" trip?'

'Wait for Farnaby and pick them all up together,' said Nick.

Leo shook her head. 'I think we should leave Farnaby alone for the time being.'

'But we've got everything we need to put him away,' Nick protested, 'especially if we can catch him actually in possession of the stuff.'

'I know,' said Leo, 'but Stone's right when he says Zahran is top priority. If he's back in the country there must be something big brewing up. We may be able to find out where he is from those two but apart from that Farnaby's our only link with him.'

'Do you think he might be at Swancombe?' Stone asked.

'Not very likely, is it?' Nick replied. 'Those three who jumped us were keeping well out of sight until Farnaby had gone. My guess is they don't want Farnaby to know where he is—or even perhaps who he is.'

'I'm inclined to agree with Nick,' Stone said.

'Just the same,' Leo persisted, 'if you arrest Farnaby Zahran will know that his men didn't finish you off and he'll be on his guard. Better to leave Farnaby for the time being. There's always the chance that Zahran, or whoever he's working for, plans to use him again. You get back to London with those two and put Pascoe in the picture. I'll stay close to Farnaby.'

'You mean you're going back to the house?' Stone frowned at her doubtfully.

'Why not? When Farnaby left I was fast asleep, thanks to whatever it was he put in my tea. When he gets back I shall just be waking up. There's no reason why he should suspect that I've ever been out of bed.'

'Unless someone has checked up on you,' Nick suggested.

Leo shrugged. 'I left some pillows in the bed—good enough to fool someone just looking in from the door. I'll have to take a chance on it.'

Stone shook his head. 'I don't like it.'

'Whether you like it or not isn't important,' she told him crisply; then her mouth softened. 'Look, I shall go back to town later today just as he expects. I know he's coming back too because I heard him making a date with someone for this evening. I'll just carry on exactly as before, keeping tabs on him. You get on with looking for Zahran. I'll keep in touch through Pascoe.' She rose. 'Where's your car?'

'Hidden by some farm buildings up on the main road,' Stone said. 'I'll go and fetch it. You keep an eye on those two, Nick. Do you want us to drop you, Leo—if you insist on going back?'

She grinned. 'No thanks. I've got my own transport.'

They walked with her to the edge of the landing-stage. She said,

'By the way, did you get the girl settled OK, Nick?'

'Yes,' he told her. 'They'll look after her at the clinic—and I contacted the parents.'

They paused above the point where the dinghy was moored. The two men looked at Leo, then glanced at each other. Stone said,

'I guess we owe you, Leo.'

She smiled. 'Don't worry. I'll think of something.'

They watched her scramble down into the boat and take up the oars.

'Why don't you use the engine?' Nick asked. 'You've got a long pull back against the current.'

Leo looked at the outboard wistfully and sighed.

'No, it's too risky. Better get back as silently as I came.

Stone untied the mooring line and dropped it into the bows. Leo tugged at the oars and the boat moved away into the middle of the stream. They waited until the faint splash of the oars was no longer audible. Then Stone said,

'That is one tough lady!'

'Yeah,' Nick said thoughtfully. 'The remarkable thing is—she's also a bloody marvellous...' he hesitated.

'Cook?' Stone offered.

'Yeah. That as well,' Nick agreed.

Stone turned and caught his eye and they both grinned. Then they walked back towards the boat-house.

Chapter 8

Nick suppressed a yawn, flexed tense muscles in his shoulders and rubbed a hand cautiously across the back of his neck. This was Tuesday. He had scarcely been to bed over the weekend and a snatched six hours the previous night had done little to make up the deficit. Added to that, his head still hurt where he had been hit. He got up from the desk where he had been checking through reports of sightings of men who might have answered to Zahran's description and went to join Pascoe and Stone.

They were standing in the control room from which all Triple S operations were directed. Down the centre of the room was a bank of computer terminals, while ranged along the walls was a comprehensive selection of communications equipment—telephones, teleprinters, radios. Practically every position was occupied by a Triple S operative and almost all of them were working on locating Stratos Zahran. Pascoe looked up as Nick arrived. Nick shook his head.

'There isn't a single sighting there that looks really hopeful. I've marked the ones that might be worth following up, but I don't think they'll turn up anything.'

Pascoe allowed the computer print-out which he had been studying to drop gently from his hand onto the desk and wandered back towards his own room. The computer operator looked after him.

'Sid's not happy,' she remarked.

It was a matter of argument among Triple S agents whether it was simply Pascoe's position as head of what they referred to as 'the Snake Pit' which had earned him his nickname of Hissing Sid, or whether it was a direct reference to his own personality. Certainly there was something about the urbane manner and the silky inflections of the voice which was reminiscent of the original character, but most of his subordinates agreed that the chief reason for the name was the habit he had of listening to reports with his eyes half closed, his whole manner as somnolent as a snake basking in the sun, until some slight inaccuracy, some bit of woolly thinking, was seized upon with the deadly rapidity of a striking cobra.

'Well, you know why, don't you?' Stone asked, picking up the computer print-out. 'Because all this adds up to precisely nothing. We're no further forward than we were this time yesterday.'

The door of Pascoe's office reopened.

'If I could interrupt you two gentlemen at your meditations for a moment...' The voice was at its smoothest.

Stone and Marriot exchanged a quick glance and followed him into the other room. Pascoe seated himself behind his desk and leaned back in his chair, his hands folded in front of his chin, elbows on the chair arms, eyelids drooping.

'So...' he said after a moment, 'Let us review the situation.'

He glanced up and made a brief gesture towards chairs on the other side of the desk. Stone and Marriot sat gratefully.

'So far,' Pascoe went on, 'we have no reports of anyone answering Zahran's description registering at any hotel or boarding-house. None of our Arab contacts seem to have any inkling of his whereabouts—or if they have they're too frightened to say anything. And he hasn't made contact with any of his known associates. However, he is obviously being looked after somewhere.'

'My guess is they've got him stashed away in a private house somewhere,' Stone said. 'If he's got someone to fetch and carry—do the shopping and so on—there's no reason why he should show his face outside until the time comes to do whatever it is he's here to do.'

'And what is he here to do?' ruminated Pascoe. 'That is the question.'

'Are we making any progress with the two men we brought in?' Nick asked.

Pascoe sighed. 'Our experts are leaning on them—but what can you expect? They've been trained by people to whom torture and mutilation are part of a way of life. They're not going to be frightened by anything we can do to them. Oh, we shall break them in the end— our methods make up in sophistication what they lack in brutality—but it will take time. And time is something we may have very little of.'

'So, what do we try next?' Stone asked.

The heavy eyelids lifted and Pascoe met his eyes. 'There are always two ends to a piece of string, Stone. The one we were following may have disappeared into the tangle for the moment, but we can always look for the other one.'

'You mean Zahran's target?' Nick suggested.

'Precisely,' agreed Pascoe.

'But that could be anyone of several hundred people,' Stone objected. 'We know from past experience that Zahran's not particularly choosy about who he knocks off, as long as the money's right.'

'I think we can narrow the field considerably from that number,' Pascoe said meditatively. 'After all, we know who brought him in. His current masters are the same people who have been supplying Farnaby with drugs; and we know that one of their agents was Ahmed Khalil. Khalil, we have good reason to believe, was involved in blowing up Sheik Mahoud, who was here on a trade mission, the outcome of which was that his country was to receive a considerable quantity of our latest and most sophisticated armaments. In return he had guaranteed his support in our efforts to obtain a settlement of the Arab-Israeli conflict. I think we can conclude, therefore, that whoever is behind Khalil and Zahran is opposed to our Government's position with regard to that settlement.'

'You mean the PLO,' said Stone succinctly.

'Them, or someone who sympathizes with them.'

'Gadhafi?' suggested Nick.

'The precise entity is not important,' Pascoe commented. 'What we are interested in is the object of their intentions.'

'Someone prominent in the Jewish community?' Nick offered. 'Someone with Zionist connections.'

'But why now? Why at this precise point in time?' Pascoe asked. 'I think we need to be more topical in our thinking. What is happening next week which is relevant to what we are discussing?' Then, as they both hesitated, 'Come, come, you read the papers— I hope.'

'We haven't had a lot of time for reading lately,' Stone said pointedly.

Pascoe ignored the comment.

'Got it!' Nick exclaimed. 'Conference of all the interested parties, starting Tuesday in Geneva.'

'Precisely,' Pascoe said, with a gentle sibilance that recalled his nickname.

'So you reckon Zahran is over here to get at someone who can affect that conference?' Stone looked dubious. 'It's hard to see how.'

'I admit that,' Pascoe agreed, 'but I think the idea is worth pursuing.'

'Who is our delegate at the conference?' Nick asked.

'The Foreign Secretary himself.'

'Would there be any advantage to the PLO if he was—unable to attend, for any reason?'

'Not so far as I can see,' Pascoe lifted his shoulders. 'A delay, perhaps, if their action caused some reorganization among the Government benches; but not a change in policy. After all, it is a Cabinet decision and there is only one person in the Cabinet whose views really carry any weight.'

'The PM,' said Stone.

'Could that be who they're aiming for?' Nick asked.

'It is possible, I suppose; but it's hard to see what they could hope to gain in the long run, except a hardening of attitudes.'

'Unless they could pin the blame on the other side,' Stone murmured, thinking aloud.

'Or unless they reckoned on getting someone more sympathetic to their views instead,' Nick suggested.

Pascoe sighed and shook his head. 'It doesn't feel right. Something doesn't add up. Still, it's the nearest thing to a lead we've got at the moment. We'll warn everyone concerned to tighten up on routine security and meanwhile we'll just have to go on keeping our ears to the ground and hope to pick up some vibrations.' He looked at the two men in front of him. 'You two look about as alert as a couple of dead ferrets. Go home, for God's sake, get some sleep; and come back when you don't need matchsticks to prop your eyes open.'

They rose, but Stone lingered. 'Has Leo been in contact today?' he asked at length.

Pascoe looked at him, his head tilted slightly on one side.

'She came in for a short while this morning. Of course, you knew she was back in London. She told me you both telephoned last night.'

Stone caught Nick's eyes briefly and looked away.

'Don't you think we ought to be keeping an eye on her—now more than ever?'

'Oh quite,' agreed Pascoe smoothly. 'But I take the point you made a few days ago. In the present situation I can't afford to waste experienced agents like you two on "baby-minding". I've assigned someone else to watch over Miss Cavendish—from a discreet distance, of course.'

'From a discreet distance!' Stone muttered, as they walked down the corridor towards the lift. 'It had bloody well better be, otherwise when I find out who it is I'll…'

He left the sentence unfinished. 'Yeah,' agreed Nick, 'so will I.'

They were both back in Pascoe's office at nine that evening. There had been no further progress in locating Zahran and Pascoe's eyelids were drooping more heavily than ever.

'What about the two birds we brought in?' Stone asked. 'Have they started to sing yet?'

'Not to any tune we want to hear,' Pascoe replied. 'We know a little more than we did, but it doesn't help us greatly. The English one is known to Special Branch as one of the leaders of a neo-Fascist organization which calls itself the "Sons of Empire"; though what they hope to gain from shacking up with the PLO we have yet to discover.'

'What nationality is the other one?' Nick asked.

'His passport says Cypriot, but we suspect he is probably Palestinian.'

'I was just wondering…' Nick murmured. 'Did we tell you that Leo spoke to him in his own language—I suppose it was his own language?'

Pascoe pursed his lips. 'Oh, quite probably. That might have been Arabic, Turkish, Demotic Greek—or any one of a number of Middle Eastern languages. She's fluent in several.'

Stone took a pace or two forward, leaned on the back of a

chair and fixed Pascoe with an unwavering stare.

'Tell me,' he said, 'apart from triple somersaults off a high wire, is there anything she doesn't do?' Then he stepped back and made a quick negating movement with his hand. 'No, don't tell me—she actually grew up in a circus and she's been an accomplished trapeze artist since the age of 5.'

Pascoe gave one of his rare chuckles. 'Not so far as I know. But she is an accomplished linguist. Which isn't surprising considering it was her original field of study.'

'In what sense?' Nick asked, eager to extract any information while Pascoe was in an expansive mood.

'When she left school she went up to Oxford to read modern languages.'

'You mean she has a degree from Oxford as well,' said Stone heavily.

'No.' Pascoe paused and Nick sensed that he felt he had said too much. 'No, she left the university before taking her degree.'

Nick would have liked to press the conversation further but there was something about the way his chief's mouth had closed on the last sentence that told him it would be useless.

Pascoe was sorting through some papers on his desk.

'I've gone through those possible sightings which you marked,' he said, 'and there are two others which have come in since which also seem worth following up. I want you two to go and check them out on the spot, since you have seen Zahran more recently than anyone else. They're fairly well dispersed—Bristol, Chichester, Essex, the far side of Birmingham and beyond. Divide them between you. If you get on the road tonight you should be able to start making enquiries first thing in the morning.'

* * *

It was late afternoon when Nick got back. He found Stone seated behind the desk in a spare office, reading a computer print-out. He looked up as Nick came in.

'Any luck?'

Nick shook his head. 'Not even the faintest sniff of the old fox. You?'

'No, nothing. Complete waste of time.'

Nick indicated the print-out. 'Got something useful there?'

'Not useful exactly,' Stone said thoughtfully. 'Interesting.'

Nick dropped into a chair on the other side of the desk, took off his jacket and eased his arm out of the shoulder holster. 'How long have you been back?' he asked.

'About an hour.'

'How come you always get to finish before me?' Nick complained.

Stone looked up and grinned. 'Greater efficiency.'

'You mean you break more speed limits,' retorted his partner. Then, 'Well, come on— interest me. I could do with something to stimulate my mind.'

Stone leaned back in his chair and narrowed his eyes. 'I'm not sure that this is something I want to tell you about.'

'So wait till next time you want me to change shifts with you or something…' Nick returned.

Stone sighed. 'OK, OK. What does the name Frank Wainwright mean to you?'

'Nothing,' said Nick blankly. 'Should it?'

'Suppose I add "Oxford—1973"?'

'Good God,' said Nick. 'That's a bit before my time!'

'Yes, well,' Stone replied, his voice heavily weighted with irony, 'I appreciate that you were hardly out of nappies—' he moved his feet neatly to avoid the kick which Nick aimed at him under the desk—'but it was rather before mine too.'

'So?' queried Nick.

Stone looked at the printout. 'Frank Wainwright was a biologist doing postgraduate research into genetic engineering. His work had a potential application to biological warfare. In November 1973 he was suspected of and subsequently proved to have been, passing on his results to the Russians; but before any action could be taken against him he committed suicide, which is why the matter never came to court.'

Nick looked puzzled. 'I still don't see how this is relevant.'

'I didn't say it was relevant,' Stone returned. 'I said it was interesting.'

'In what way, interesting?'

Stone shook his head despairingly. 'Oxford,' he said slowly. '1973. Pascoe said Leo went up to Oxford immediately after leaving school, so that would have been...?'

Nick did a rapid calculation. 'About that time! But apart from the fact that they were both at Oxford at the same time, what makes you think there was a connection?'

'Wainwright didn't give himself away, and he wasn't found out through the usual security channels,' said Stone. 'He was stopped—by a woman; a student who was also his girl-friend. A woman who is referred to in the file simply as "Miss C."'

Nick gazed at him for a moment in silence. 'What put you on to this?'

'I got to thinking, on the long, boring drive home. Didn't it strike you that Pascoe knew more than he was telling us about why Leo left without completing her degree? So when I got back and found he was out and I had a few minutes to spare I got Penny in the computer room to turn up anything she could find with an Oxford connection during the relevant years—and she came up with this.'

'So are you saying that Leo's been working for Triple S ever since then?'

'Could be.'

'Does the file say what happened to "Miss C."?'

'That's the really interesting bit,' Stone said quietly. 'It simply records that all further information has been transferred to a separate file, coded for the director or his deputy only.'

'In other words, to a Triple S operative's personal record file,' Nick said.

'Exactly!' cut in a voice from the door. 'A file to which you, quite rightly, have no access.'

They both rose and swung round to face Pascoe. His face was a mask.

'Come through to my room,' he said curtly, and turned on his heel.

They followed him in silence and stood waiting while he settled himself behind his desk and looked from one to the other. Nick saw the steely glint beneath the lowered eyelids and the telltale tightening of his partner's jaw and prepared himself for a bumpy ride.

'It is a pity,' Pascoe began at length, 'that you two have not been devoting the same detective powers to the operation in hand as you obviously have to the personal history of one of your fellow operatives. I'm quite sure that you, Stone, would be the first to insist that anything that may be known to me about an agent's life prior to joining Triple S should be a matter of total confidence.' Stone made a move as if to protest and Pascoe silenced him with a gesture. 'I know, you are about to tell me that the computer record which you were studying was simply one of a previous operation and one to which your security coding gave you access without reference to any higher authority.' He paused. 'I am also prepared to admit that it was something which I let slip which first put you on to it. Nevertheless, in other circumstances I would simply tell you to let the matter drop there and make no further inquiries; but as it is—' he paused again, as if reluctant to continue—'I propose to tell you the rest of the story; not to satisfy your curiosity, but to protect her and to ensure, as far as I can, that neither of you open any old wounds by asking too many questions.'

He gestured to the two chairs in front of the desk. Stone and Marriot sat, glancing at each other uneasily.

'I hope I don't need to emphasize the fact that nothing I am going to tell you must ever be repeated,' Pascoe went on. 'And that neither of you must ever give the faintest sign to Leonora herself that you know any more than she may choose to tell you.' They both nodded silently. Pascoe folded his hands in his usual manner in front of his chin and appeared for a moment to be collecting his thoughts.

'Leonora went up to Oxford in 1972,' he began. 'She had an excellent academic record at school and every prospect of a brilliant career ahead of her. She came from a very respectable, middle-class family and had been educated at a fairly exclusive girls' day-school. Her life up to that point had been, shall we say, sheltered. Shortly after going up she became involved with Wainwright who was, by all accounts, brilliant but highly unstable. They became lovers. Towards the beginning of her second year she began to suspect that he was passing secrets to the other side. Being the person she is, she said nothing but set about obtaining irrefutable proof. It took her until November. It so happened that a niece of mine had been a school friend of Leonora's and that we had met once at my niece's home. Leo knew that I had some connection with security, though not, of course, precisely what; but when she had her proof and wanted someone to pass it on to I suppose I must have seemed the obvious choice. She got my address from my niece and wrote me a letter setting out her grounds for suspicion and citing her proofs. It was a most impressive document. She posted it on a Thursday and when I received it on the Friday I immediately prepared to follow it up, though it wasn't strictly speaking a Triple S matter. However, I was already too late. Apparently, on the Thursday evening she went to Wainwright's laboratory, where he was working late, alone, and told him what she had done. It's not hard to understand why. Her conscience wouldn't allow her to stand by and see thousands of lives put at risk. On the other hand, she had been, perhaps still was, in love with the man. She was giving him one faint chance of getting away. Unfortunately, as I said earlier, he was a very unstable character. Either he panicked, or it was a last spiteful attempt to punish her—I don't know. He grabbed the nearest bottle of lethal chemical and managed to swallow enough of it to kill himself, though very far from instantly. The laboratory was empty, apart from the two of them. Leo screamed for help but it was some time before the caretaker heard her. There was nothing she could do but watch him die, a slow and agonizing death.' Nick put the back of his hand against his mouth and pressed his lips very hard against it. He glanced at Stone, but his eyes were firmly fixed on the carpet between his feet.

'It's an ugly story,' Pascoe said quietly, 'but I'm afraid it gets worse. Three weeks later she realized that she was pregnant—she was carrying Wainwright's child.'

There was a long silence. Stone got up abruptly and went to stand with his back to them, looking out of the window.

'What did she do?' Nick asked at length.

'She gave up her university course and went abroad. All that winter she worked in a hotel in Switzerland. Came back speaking nearly perfect French and German and found a job as a translator which kept her going until the baby was born. It was offered for adoption—I believe she never even saw it. As soon as she was strong enough she went abroad again— Italy, Greece, Cyprus, Turkey, Israel, Egypt— doing a variety of jobs; waitress, nanny, companion-secretary. That's how she knows the domestic service trade so well. She picked up the languages of all the countries she worked in, with half a dozen local dialects on the side. At the end of two years she felt able to think about a proper career again. She'd always had a love for acting and so she decided to come back to England and apply for a place at RADA. By the end of the course she was their star pupil, went straight into the Royal Shakespeare Company—and the rest is a matter of public record.'

'Hardly that, surely,' Stone said, turning away from the window. 'What made her give up acting? And when did you recruit her into Triple S?'

'That,' said Pascoe firmly, 'is a different story and one which…'

'Which she only tells to particularly close friends…' murmured Nick under his breath.

'What was that?' asked Pascoe.

'Nothing,' Nick said quickly. 'Sorry, sir.'

'Anyway,' Pascoe resumed, 'you will understand why she will never talk about that part of her life, and why you must never question her about it.'

Nick looked at Stone and then at Pascoe.

They both nodded. Stone started to speak and then had to stop and clear his throat.

'You—you can rely on us, sir. Thank you for putting us in the picture.'

'Well now,' said Pascoe. 'I hope you will be able to concentrate your minds on finding Stratos Zahran. Here is a list of suspected PLO sympathizers in London. Get out there and lean on them—hard!'

* * *

Late that night Leo called Pascoe on his personal line. 'Nothing very definite, I'm afraid,' she said, 'but I think we ought to follow it up. You've heard about this big exhibition that the Sports Council are organizing at Olympia—something to do with making the most of your increased leisure time?'

'In other words, how to occupy the unemployed,' Pascoe commented drily. 'Yes, I read something about it. Why?'

'There's going to be a big reception tomorrow night to inaugurate it and Farnaby's wangled himself an invitation. The curious thing is, Guy Farnaby feels faint at the prospect of anything more energetic than a strenuous game of backgammon. The only possible reason he could have for going is because there is going to be someone there he's interested in. Can you get a sight of the guest list?'

'Of course,' Pascoe agreed. 'Come in tomorrow morning and we'll go through it.'

When Leo arrived the next morning Pascoe greeted her with, 'I think we may be on to something. The powers that be obviously want to give this thing maximum publicity. The guest list for tonight is extremely high-powered. Apart from the usual sports celebrities and TV personalities there are representatives from practically every embassy in London, MPs from all parties and several members of the Government—including the Prime Minister and family.'

Leo met his eyes. 'Sounds like Triple S ought to be represented too, don't you think?'

Half an hour later Nick arrived in response to a summons from Control. Leo had already left.

'Ah, Marriot,' said Pascoe. 'You had a fairly chequered career before you joined the police. Did you ever work as a waiter?'

Nick blinked. 'Once or twice, for short periods.'

'Good, then today should give you no problems. For the next twenty-four hours you are an employee of the Cavendish Domestic Agency. Report there for training straight away.'

Nick arrived at the agency whistling happily but if he had supposed that his 'training' would be a mere formality he was soon disillusioned. The Cavendish Agency worked on the principle that all its staff were of the highest possible calibre and Leo was not about to have its reputation spoiled by anyone, even a Triple S agent. Nick found himself handed over to a gentleman called Mr Burrows who had started life as an RSM and had then served as a butler in some of the most distinguished houses in the country and who now enlivened his retirement by taking on an occasional assignment for the Cavendish Agency. It was very soon made clear to Nick that his ideas of the correct behaviour for a waiter were not the same as Mr Burrows's; and his discomfiture was not lessened by the fact that Helen, the blonde secretary, kept remarking that she was sure they had met before, somewhere. When Leo sent him out to get his hair cut it was almost the last straw.

He was considerably comforted, however, by the discovery that Leo would be working alongside him that evening.

'I would have thought you'd be going along with Farnaby,' he commented.

She shook her head. 'It was made very clear to me last night that my presence was not required. He kept telling me how boring I should find it.'

'It's a bit risky for you to be there at all then, isn't it?' he objected. 'Suppose he recognizes you.'

She grinned. 'Don't worry. By the time I'm ready even you won't recognize me.'

'Do you fancy taking a small bet on that?' he asked, laughing.

'All right.' She looked at him quizzically. 'How about the same amount as you won off Stone the other day when we first met?'

'You don't miss much, do you,' he marvelled, still laughing. 'OK. You're on—a fiver.'

They agreed to meet in the booking-hall of the tube station, since Leo pointed out that people who went out to earn extra money as casual waiters did not normally arrive for work in a posh motor—or even in a taxi. Nick arrived a few minutes before the appointed time and looked around him. The booking-hall was empty except for a dark-haired woman in a rather short black skirt and a cheap fake fur coat standing with her back to him apparently studying a map on the wall. Nick grinned to himself and moved over towards her. The height was right, if you allowed for those ridiculously high heels; and that hair was surely a wig. He closed in behind her and cleared his throat.

'Excuse me, madam, but I think you owe me five pounds.'

'You what?'

She turned and he found himself staring into opaque brown eyes. Under the thick make-up he could see that the skin was sallow and the eyelids puffy and discoloured, and when she smiled the teeth were stained with nicotine. He stepped back sharply.

'I'm sorry! I thought you were somebody else. Sorry...'

He beat a hasty retreat and paced up and down the far side of the booking-hall, watching the up escalator and praying for Leo to arrive. Five minutes passed. He reflected that he would not have expected her to be unpunctual. Then he saw that the woman was coming towards him and his heart sank at the thought that she was going to try and pick him up. She took a cigarette out of a case as she approached and put it between her lips.

'Got a light, love?' The voice was throaty and the articulation slack.

'Sorry,' he said again. 'I don't smoke.'

She took the cigarette out of her mouth and smiled and for the first time he noticed the sweet curve of the lips.

'No,' she said softly, 'nor do I unless I'm absolutely forced to.'

'Leo?' he said incredulously.

'I think you owe me five pounds,' she replied.

'But it's unbelievable!' he exclaimed. 'How do you do it?'

'Tricks of the trade, love,' she said with a grin. 'But of course the contact lenses are the most vital part. Come on, we're going to be late.'

Once again Nick found that working for Cavendish was not an easy option. He had assumed that all he would have to do was wander round with a tray of drinks and keep his eyes open; but the manager from the catering company who were in charge of the refreshments for the reception had no idea that Nick and Leo were any different from the other casual help which had been employed from various sources and Nick soon found himself set to work unpacking and polishing glasses. Once the guests began to arrive he was busier than ever and it seemed that every time he paused to have a look round the manager appeared at his elbow and demanded to know why he was standing about when there were people without a glass in their hands. At last, when the first rush was over and he was able to draw breath, he spotted Leo standing by one of the buffet tables. As he made his way towards her he thought how completely right she looked with the neat little white apron over the slightly too short dress and her air of tawdry sophistication.

Just as he reached her there was a flurry of activity by the main entrance as the Prime Minister's party arrived. Under cover of the general hubbub Nick said,

'Spotted anything?'

Leo shook her head. 'If Zahran's here then I haven't seen him. Mind you, with this many people around it wouldn't be hard to miss him.'

'Well,' Nick said, 'the building has been searched, and Stone and his team are covering all the entrances and watching it all on closed- circuit TV, so they may spot anything we've missed. Where's Farnaby?'

'Over there,' Leo said, nodding. 'With that little bunch of TV celebrities. If you want to find Farnaby just look for someone with a name. He can't resist anyone rich or famous. That's why he likes to be seen around with me. Look, I daren't get too close, just in case. Why don't you wander over and see if you can pick up anything?'

Nick did as she suggested. It was not easy to overhear any one conversation in the general noise but by straining his ears he managed to pick up the general drift of what was being said. There was nothing in it of any significance, as far as he could tell. Before long he saw the manager heading in his direction again and decided he had better get on with handing round the drinks. A little later he passed Leo.

'Have you noticed who Farnaby's latched onto now?' she murmured.

Nick looked round. 'Who?'

'On the left there.'

Nick frowned at the fair-haired young man who had joined the group. 'I know the face, but I'm damned if I can think who he is.'

Leo clicked her tongue disapprovingly. 'You haven't been doing your homework. That, my unobservant friend, is the PM's son. Better keep an eye on them.'

Nick managed to hover in the general area of the little group for the next half-hour or so. The young man seemed to find Farnaby very congenial and Nick had the impression that Farnaby was deliberately setting out to charm him, but at length he rejoined the Prime Minister and shortly afterwards the party left. That was the sign for the gathering to begin to break up. Nick heaved a sigh of relief and became aware that his feet were aching. It struck him that Stone had had the best job, watching the whole thing on TV. At least he would have been able to sit down. Sitting down seemed like a good idea, but he had hardly formulated it when he found himself hard at work again, collecting glasses, drying them and repacking them. It was another hour before he and Leo finally made their way back to the tube station. She smiled at him.

'Fancy a nightcap?'

'I don't know about a nightcap,' he commented. 'I could do with a bloody good meal. I'm starving.'

'Well, I expect there's something in the freezer,' she said.

'No,' he said. 'This time I'll take you out.'

'Looking like this?' she queried ironically.

'I don't give a damn how you look,' he said.

'Give me five minutes,' she said, and disappeared into the ladies' room.

This time he was prepared for the transformation but he would still hardly have recognized her if it had not been for the fact that she was still wearing the cheap coat. The wig had gone, and the contact lenses, and the thick make-up had disappeared. She looked fresh and scrubbed and very appealing. He caught her hand.

'To hell with the tube. Let's get a taxi.'

He took her to his favourite Italian restaurant in the Kings

Road and took pleasure in watching her tuck into polio alia cacciatora. He knew that if he had brought her here as Leonora Carr the waiters would have been falling over themselves and people at the other tables would have been watching them and asking each other who *he* was; but he preferred her like this, with her short hair tousled and her face almost without make-up. Over the zabaglione he said,

'Can I ask you something?'

She looked up and raised an eyebrow. 'Mmn?'

These different parts you play all the time... I don't mean tonight because that was just for a couple of hours, and obviously quite different from you; but the roles you seem to play all the time—Laura Cavendish, Leonora Carr... Don't you ever feel, well, confused?'

She sat back and smiled at him. 'Will the real Leonora please stand up, you mean?' She considered for a moment. 'Occasionally, I suppose; but not seriously. I know who I am—and it isn't either of them. Leonora Carr was me, once. I only changed my name when I joined Equity because my agent told me that a shorter name was easier to fit on programmes and posters and things. But she stopped being me after that film. For a while I never wanted to hear of her again. Now she's just a fictitious character as far as I'm concerned.'

'You really hate that film, don't you,' he said.

'Deeply and passionately,' she agreed.

'But why? I mean, it was a tremendous success. It made you famous all over the world.'

'You saw it?' she asked and he nodded. 'Remember how it made you feel about me,' she commented, 'and then ask yourself if that's how you would like to be thought of.'

After a moment he said, 'Is that why you left Hollywood?'

'Largely.'

In the pause he ordered coffee and brandy. When the waiter had gone he said,

'Tell me one thing. You said that you had convinced Farnaby that you left Hollywood because you had got mixed up with the drugs scene out there and wanted to kick the habit. It wasn't true, was it?'

She reached out and put her hand over his. 'No, my sweet. I left partly because I couldn't bear to watch what it was doing to a lot of the people I met; but I was never involved myself. I never have been.'

'I'm glad,' he murmured. 'I wouldn't have asked but…'

'I know,' she interrupted him gently. 'Stone told me, while you were taking care of Mandy. I'm sorry about Jacky—that was her name, wasn't it.'

He squeezed her fingers. 'It was a long time ago now—water under the bridge. I just can't bear to think of it happening again to anyone—anyone I care about.'

The coffee arrived. Nick sat back.

'So—what does the real Leonora do with herself at weekends? When she isn't paddling about rivers at the dead of night, that is.'

She sipped her coffee. 'I have a tiny cottage in a hollow of the North Downs in Surrey, and I keep a horse at livery at a stable nearby. When I get the chance I go down and ride. It's only twenty-five miles from London, but if you know your way about you can ride all day without touching a main road.'

He grinned. 'I should have known you rode horses.'

She gave him a steady look. 'To be a good horseman takes patience, sensitivity, courage and a fair degree of physical fitness, so I shall take that as a compliment; though I suspect it isn't quite what you had in mind.'

'What's it called—your horse?' he asked.

'I call him Dippy,' she said. 'His name is Serendipity.'

'Funny name for a horse.'

'Not really. His dam was called Serenade and he's by a stallion called Lucky Chance— so, Serendipity. It means a happy chance.'

'What else do you do, in your tiny cottage?'

'Read, listen to music…'

'What sort of music?'

'Strictly classical, I'm afraid—Bach, Mozart, Beethoven. Not your scene?'

'Very much my scene,' he contradicted her. He cradled his brandy glass, looking at her. 'And you do these things all alone?'

Her eyes met his over the rim of her glass. 'Yes—quite alone.'

Later he walked her home along the embankment. The warm weather was continuing and the dark river, at full flood, mirrored the necklace of fairy lights across the Albert Bridge. He glanced sideways at her and remembered what Pascoe had told them; and reached out and took her hand.

When they stood at the door of her flat she smiled up at him. 'How about that nightcap now?'

'That sounds like a wonderful idea,' he said, and followed her inside.

* * *

The following morning Nick and Stone met for a conference in Pascoe's office.

'So,' Pascoe remarked. 'Nothing happened last night.'

'Nothing,' said Stone. 'Complete waste of time.'

'Oh, I wouldn't say that,' Nick murmured.

'You wouldn't? Why not?' Pascoe demanded.

'Well, I mean—' Nick floundered, his brain racing out of gear—'we had to be there, didn't we? I mean, we couldn't risk not being.'

'That is true,' Pascoe agreed. 'We had to take all due precautions, under the circumstances.'

'Do you reckon Zahran may have been planning something and called it off because he spotted us?' Stone asked.

Pascoe shook his head. 'Unlikely. It's not his style to be put off by the sight of opposition.'

'Maybe Farnaby was there on some ploy of his own, completely unconnected with Zahran,' Nick suggested.

'That is certainly a possibility,' Pascoe agreed. 'You say he spent some time with the PM's son?'

'Yes. I should say he was making a definite effort to get friendly with him.'

'Well,' Pascoe brooded, 'bearing in mind the way he used Amanda Clifton we can't discount the idea that he may be hoping to compromise the boy in some way for his own devious ends.'

'On the other hand,' Nick put in, 'he may just have been basking in reflected glory. Leo says he can't resist anyone with any claim to fame.'

Pascoe sighed. 'I think all we can hope for is that we have got hold of one more piece of the jigsaw. We may not be able to recognize it at the moment, but with any luck it will suddenly click into place when we begin to see the whole picture. One thing is certain, anyway, we're not going to see it any clearer sitting in this office. Get out on the streets and start asking questions. Somebody, somewhere, must know something.'

Going off duty at the end of the day Nick felt he knew no more than he had when he started. The events of the day blended into a vague impression of sleazy bars, grubby bedsitters and raucous amusement halls. It occurred to him that it would be nice to ring Leo and suggest that they went to a concert; then he remembered that she had told him that she was going to the theatre with Farnaby. It crossed his mind that he had not been in touch with either of his regular girl-friends for over a week. He wondered whether to phone one of them, but the idea did not appeal. He reached for his radio microphone, guessing that somewhere in the city Stone would also be making his way home, and gave his call sign.

'Delta One,' came the laconic reply. 'Anything?'

'Bugger all!' replied Nick. 'You?'

'No, not a murmur.'

'You got any plans for this evening?' Nick asked.

There was a brief silence, then, 'I'm not sure…'

'Leo's going out with Farnaby,' said Nick, reading his mind.

'Ah,' said Stone, non-committally. Then, 'No, I haven't got anything planned. You got any ideas?'

'Not really.'

'Fancy dropping into the Red Cow to see if there's any fresh talent around?'

'No. Not tonight.'

A pause. 'No, can't say I'm all that keen either.'

'Sky are giving a concert at the Festival Hall

'Leave it out. You know I can't sit still for a whole evening listening to music.'

There was a silence, filled with the crackling of two receivers, both listening out. Then Nick pressed his transmit button.

'Haven't been to the pictures for a long time.'

'No.' Stone considered the idea. 'What's on?'

'Have you seen ET?'

'Do me a favour!'

'Well—everybody's talking about it. I just thought...'

Stone chuckled. 'Yeah, OK. Why not? It ought to be good for a laugh.'

So they went to see ET—but neither of them laughed.

Chapter 9

Nick was just making his early morning coffee when the phone rang.

'Mr Pascoe would like to see you in his office straight away,' said Control.

He met Stone in the foyer and they went up in the lift together. Leo was already in Pascoe's room, her cheeks flushed from exercise and her hair damp from the shower. Looking at her, Nick felt pallid and unwholesome. He and Stone had sat up late the night before, after the film, drinking and talking. Neither of them had mentioned Leo, though they had known that she was uppermost in both their minds.

'I think we may be on to something,' Pascoe began without preamble. 'Tell them, Leo.'

Leo's voice was businesslike. 'Farnaby told me last night that he wouldn't be able to see me over the weekend because he was going to be "busy". Then, later on, I overheard him telling someone that he was going to be at Epsom this afternoon, for the racing. Well, Guy Farnaby is to horse-racing what Mary Whitehouse is to a Soho strip-joint; so the only possible explanation, once again, is that there is going to be somebody there that he's interested in. The question is, who.'

'Oh, only about 5,000 other people,' Stone muttered. 'Like the other night.'

'Think, Stone!' Pascoe chided him. 'Who did Farnaby meet that night?'

'Of course!' Nick exclaimed. 'The PM's son. Is he going to be there?'

'Unfortunately official sources are unable to confirm or deny that,' Pascoe replied. 'As a private citizen he is under no obligation to keep us informed, and it appears that he did not spend last night at his flat and no one knows where to get in touch with him.'

'So it's another wait and watch job,' said Stone.

'I'm afraid that is about all we can do,' Pascoe agreed.

'I still don't see where this connects with Zahran,' Nick put in. 'OK, there might be something in it for Farnaby, with his nasty little habits, but where's the political mileage for a terrorist like Zahran?'

'I can only assume through bringing pressure to bear on the PM,' said Pascoe.

'Then it is a blackmail job,' commented Stone.

'It may be a red herring, for all we know,' sighed Pascoe. 'But once again, it's one we can't afford not to follow up. We shall go on looking for Zahran and maintaining precautions in other directions, of course. But I want you three on this job, so let's get down to some planning. We've got three hours, and a lot of ground to cover—in every sense of the word.'

* * *

Stone watched the winner of the last race thunder past the post and was glad that he had decided that betting while on duty was not a good idea. However, someone else had been betting, and with remarkable success. If Farnaby was as much a stranger to racing as Leo had implied, then someone had been giving him some very good tips—tips he had been sharing with a friend! Already the two of them were on their way to collect their winnings on the last race. Stone followed at a discreet distance and saw them turn in the direction of the car-park. He drew back into a doorway of the stand building and took out his radio.

'Delta One to Watchdog.'

In a plain van parked on the crest of the Downs Nick pressed down a key. 'Delta One, this is Watchdog. Go ahead.'

'It looks as if Father Bear is about ready to go home—and Goldilocks is with him.'

'Roger, Delta One. Maintain observation.' Stone left the doorway. The crowds were beginning to stream out of the stands and enclosures, heading for the car parks or strolling away across the Downs in the late afternoon sun. Stone ran up a short flight of steps at the back of the stand, from the top of which he had a fairly clear view of Farnaby's Rolls. Farnaby himself and the Prime Minister's son were talking to a small group of friends. Then Stone saw the young man reach into the boot of his car and produce a small suitcase. With a nod and a wave he and Farnaby began to move away towards the Rolls. Stone pressed the transmit button on his radio.

'Watchdog, Delta One. I think we may be onto something. It looks as if Goldilocks is going to stay with Father Bear.'

Thank you, Delta One. We have a mobile unit standing by to follow.'

Stone leaned forward suddenly as a movement caught his eye. A familiar figure in a white trouser suit had appeared between the parked cars and intercepted Farnaby and his companion. He saw her make a gesture as if to throw her arms about Farnaby's neck and saw him flinch and catch her wrist, holding her off. Stone raised his binoculars and watched the scene unfold. Leo was speaking earnestly, even tearfully, and Farnaby was plainly embarrassed. Then she seemed to grow angry and even made a gesture as if to strike him but when he turned away towards the car she ran after him and caught his sleeve, pleading with him. He jerked his arm free and the chauffeur opened the door of the Rolls. She continued her supplications until both he and the boy were in the car, and then turned abruptly and ran off, apparently in tears. Stone saw her reach the white Jaguar from the Triple S car pool which she habitually used in her ex-film-star persona and get in. 'What the hell was all that about?' he muttered to himself.

A couple of seconds later Leo's voice came over the radio, calm and even, but with an edge of urgency.

'Delta One, I'm following Father Bear. If you can get to the car-park entrance in time I'll pick you up.'

'Omega, this is Delta One. No need. There is a mobile unit already standing by.'

'I don't care if the Seventh Cavalry is standing by,' came the reply. 'I'm sticking with them. I just got a good look at the chauffeur. It's Stratos Zahran!'

Almost before she had finished speaking Stone was on his way down the steps. He saw the Rolls edging out of the car-park in the stream of traffic and reached the entrance just as Leo's Jag arrived, three cars behind. He leaned down and opened the driver's door.

'Move over. I'll drive.'

'You won't,' said Leo, and her eyes met his implacably. She eased her foot on the clutch and the car inched forward. 'Are you getting in or not?' she asked.

He ran round and got in beside her. The car slid out onto the road, following the Rolls. Stone reached for the microphone.

'Watchdog, this Delta One. I am mobile, following Father Bear.'

'Unnecessary, Delta One,' came Nick's reply. 'Kappa One and Two are already in position.'

'Correction. Maximum security absolutely vital. We have an ID on the driver. It's the man we've been looking for all this week. Please inform Control.'

There was a brief silence, then Nick's voice, low, as if he had forgotten that he was holding down the transmit key. 'Bloody 'ell!' Then, aloud. 'Thank you, Delta One. I will contact control and get back to you. Hold a minute— Observation post two reports target has turned left onto Leatherhead road.'

'Thank you, Watchdog. We have visual contact.'

The Jag slid round a long left-hand bend. They could see Farnaby's silver Rolls dropping into the dip ahead of them and, two cars behind it, a red Vauxhall Cavalier.

'That's our two,' Stone said. 'In the red car.'

The Rolls proceeded at a sedate pace up the farther hill, the little procession of cars following it.

'By the way,' Stone said. 'What was all that in aid of in the car-park?'

'Oh, me throwing a wobbly, you mean?' Leo said. 'I wanted a chance to get a good look at the chauffeur. I strolled past earlier on and I was pretty sure it wasn't Stringer, the usual man; but he had his cap down over his eyes, pretending to be asleep, so I couldn't see who it was. I knew he'd have to get out when Farnaby appeared, so I had to have an excuse for having followed him down here in the first place. It was a sort of double bluff, really. On the surface I was doing the jealous woman act—why had he stood me up for a whole weekend etc., but he knows quite well things aren't like that between us. He thinks I'm really desperate for a new supply of dope. I've embarrassed him, annoyed him even—but hopefully I haven't blown my cover.'

The radio crackled and Nick's voice came through.

'Delta One, I have a message from Control. You are to maintain surveillance on Father Bear but not, repeat not, under any circumstances to attempt to stop him. The safety of the passenger is of paramount importance. Control is consulting with other security forces and you are to act only under direct instructions except in an emergency. Is that understood?'

'Understood, Delta Two,' Stone replied drily. 'He wouldn't like to get the instructions written out in triplicate and witnessed by a JP, too, would he?'

Nick chuckled. 'I dunno. Shall I ask him? Report your position please.'

Stone reached for the ordnance survey map which he had already found in the glove box. Leo leaned over and took the mike from him.

'Just turning right towards the village of Ashtead, heading for the A24,' she said.

'Thank you, Omega,' came Nick's reply.

'Are you sure?' Stone asked.

She gave him a brief sideways glance. 'I should be. I grew up around here, and I still come down this way most weekends. I know every inch of the country within ten miles of Dorking.'

The Rolls led them around the Leatherhead bypass. Nick came through again on the radio.

'We think Father Bear may have noticed Kappa One and Two. I've instructed them to peel off at the next roundabout. An unmarked police car is ready to take over from them.'

At the roundabout the Rolls turned left, heading for Dorking, and they saw the red Vauxhall swing away to the right while a dark blue Sierra nosed out of a lay-by and slotted in two cars behind the Rolls. Maintaining these positions they eased through the Saturday shopping crowd in Dorking High Street and headed out towards Guildford.

'Do you reckon he's going to Swancombe?' Stone asked.

'If he is, he's taking the scenic route,' Leo commented. 'It would have been much quicker and easier to head for Esher and get on the A3.'

'What's he up to?' Stone muttered. 'Is it just some kind of elaborate plan to get the boy into a compromising situation?'

'Knowing some of Farnaby's contacts I imagine that wouldn't be difficult,' Leo said. 'But then he wouldn't need Zahran. Looks like kidnapping to me.'

Once again Nick's voice crackled over the radio.

'Omega, report your position please.'

'On the A25 heading west towards Guildford; just passed through Westcott,' Leo reported.

'Thank you, Omega. Message from Control. They are scrambling a helicopter to help with surveillance. It should be over you in about ten minutes.'

'Hold it!' Leo exclaimed. 'Rolls is turning left onto minor road leading in the direction of Friday Street. We'll keep you posted.'

They saw the police car turn and followed into a narrow lane which ran steeply downhill. Within minutes the road was running between high banks with the full-leaved beech trees arching overhead, so that the lane was full of green shadow pierced by the slanting, amber rays of the late afternoon sun.

'Now what are they playing at?' Leo muttered.

'Short cut?' Stone suggested.

Leo shook her head. 'There's nowhere they could get to down here that they couldn't have reached easier and quicker by sticking to the main roads—unless their objective is somewhere very close. This area is a maze of tiny lanes, but none of them really lead anywhere.'

They rounded a bend and abruptly Leo stepped on the brake. Ahead of them a Land Rover towing a horse-box had apparently jack-knifed coming out of a gateway and was completely blocking the road. Between them and it stood the blue Sierra, the driver in the act of getting out. The Rolls had disappeared.

Stone swore softly but Leo had already slammed the car into reverse.

'What are you doing?' he asked.

'Just pray there's nothing close behind us,' she replied tersely.

As they whined back round the bend he saw what she was aiming at. To their right another lane led off downhill.

'Does this join up?' he asked as Leo pushed the car into first and swung into it.

She nodded, concentrating hard on the road. 'Yes, but it's further. We shall have to push on.'

She reached forward and pushed down a switch on the dashboard. A high-pitched bleep pulsed through the car.

'You bugged him!' Stone said.

She grinned briefly. 'That's another thing I did while I was playing my rejected woman scene.'

This lane was, if possible, even narrower than the first. The banks flashed by and the tyres squealed as they slid into a sharp s-bend. Stone found himself bracing both feet hard against the floor.

'Stop for a minute,' he said sharply. 'I'll take over.

'You're crazy!' she replied. 'We could lose them that way.'

The car swooped into the bottom of the dip, rounded a bend in a controlled skid and snarled up the hill on the far side.

'Look,' he shouted, 'I've had experience of this kind of driving!'

She glanced at him and laughed suddenly. 'You know your trouble—you just don't like being driven by a woman!'

'I don't like being driven by anyone at this speed!' he gasped, as Leo roared up through the gears on a brief straight stretch.

'Well, hard luck!' she replied.—'It's a case of "shut your eyes and think of England".'

They topped the rise and as they hurtled down into another valley Stone saw a large farm truck, of the type used for transporting livestock, heading down the opposite hill towards them. The lane was too narrow for two cars to pass comfortably. They had no hope of getting past a truck.

'Watch out!' he yelled.

'Seen it!' Leo replied, but her foot went down on the accelerator, not the brake.

'For Christ's sake, Leo!' Stone screamed. Then, as they came to the bottom of the hill, he saw what she was aiming for. In the valley a track led off to the left and at its start the lane widened briefly, enough to allow two vehicles to pass. The truck had almost reached that point and Stone saw it brake violently as they hurtled towards it, Leo's hand hard down on the horn. He braced himself as she slammed the gear lever into third and the near-side wheels ran up onto the bank just before the turning. The car tilted wildly, then dropped down as the lane widened, bounced, crashed under some low branches as it skimmed past the tail of the truck and then roared away up the next rise.

Stone drew a deep breath. 'Remind me never to come driving with you again.'

'Get on the radio, tell them where we are,' she said.

He reached for the mike and called, 'Watchdog, this is Delta One...'

There was no reply. He tried the call sign again, with the same result.

'Could we be out of range?' Leo asked.

'Not with this equipment,' he assured her.

He wound down the window and craned his head and shoulders out to peer up at the roof.

'Hell!' he said, wriggling back in. 'We've lost our aerial. It must have got snapped off when we went under those low branches.'

Leo said nothing for a moment. Then she remarked, 'Looks like we're on our own.' Another thought occurred to Stone. He reached out and twiddled a knob on the dashboard.

'We've lost our bleep, too.'

'There's a hand-held receiver in the glove box,' she told him. 'We're almost back to the original road now. When we get there you may be able to pick them up if you get out of the car.'

The car approached a T-junction and slowed. 'This is it,' Leo said. 'They must be somewhere in this area.'

Stone took the receiver and got out. He picked up the signal from the bug almost at once.

'They're ahead of us,' he told her, 'but not very far.'

She turned right and gunned the Jag along the new road. They slanted down the escarpment of the Downs and through a gap in the trees Stone caught a flash of silver below them.

'There he is,' he said. Then, remembering, 'Where the hell is that chopper they were supposed to be sending?'

'Wondering where the hell we are, I expect,' Leo replied

'With all this tree cover he'll have a hard job spotting us. And he may well be looking for us on the wrong side of the hills. That would be our last reported position.'

A few minutes later they came within sight of the Rolls, now heading serenely out across the level ground at the foot of the Downs. Leo throttled back and the sedate forty felt like a crawl after their former speed.

'Beats me where they're heading for,' Stone murmured fretfully.

They drove in silence for a while. Then Leo said, 'Hallo, this could be it!'

The Rolls signalled left and disappeared up a long drive which led to a farmhouse and a collection of large barns. Leo stopped the car and Stone read the notice on the gatepost.

'Huntersford Farm—private property; no right of way.'

'Now what?' Leo asked.

'Good question,' he replied. 'I think you leave me here to keep an eye on things while you get to the nearest phone-box and call control.'

She nodded, and then stiffened suddenly and wound down her window.

'Listen! What's that?'

Stone put his head out of his window and listened.

'The chopper?' he suggested, but she shook her head. Then without warning she started the engine and swung the car into the drive.

'What...?' Stone began.

'Look!' she yelled. 'Over there, to the left of the barns.'

He looked. On that side of the buildings the ground was almost flat for some distance, and suddenly he saw what she was looking at. Just visible beyond the corner of a barn a windsock floated in the light breeze. Then he knew what it was they had heard. It was the sound of a light aircraft warming up.

The Jag hurtled up the drive. As they approached the house two men leapt into their path, one of them armed with a shotgun.

Stone yelled. 'Look out!' and flung his arm across his face as the windscreen shattered under a hail of pellets. Leo ducked for an instant and the car swerved wildly, then came back under control and squealed round the end of the nearest barn. Stone drew his pistol and knocked out the remaining glass. They skidded round another corner and almost collided with the parked Rolls. Beyond it was the landing-strip and, at the far end, an executive jet was turning into the wind ready for take-off.

'There!' Stone shouted, but already Leo was hurling the Jag down the runway.

'How much distance do those need to take off?' she yelled.

'Not much!' he shouted back.

The wind coming through the broken windshield lashed their faces. He glanced at the speedometer and saw it climb past eighty to ninety and then on up towards the hundred. Ahead of them the plane held on its take-off path. The gap, he reckoned, must be closing at over two hundred miles an hour. His mouth went dry as he realized Leo's intention. The jet had its nose up, but there was less than a hundred yards between them. He saw the plane tilt as the pilot tried frantically to drag it off the runway. Then the car skidded and yawed violently to the right as Leo stood on the brakes and there was a rending crash as the plane's wing-tip seared across their roof, followed by a few seconds of blessed silence as they rocked and bounced to a standstill.

Stone punched his seat-belt loose and looked round. Behind them the plane had slewed onto the grass and stood, one wing hanging like a wounded bird, the other dug into the earth. People were already clambering out of it. He turned to Leo. She was slumped across the steering-wheel, apparently unconscious. Stone kicked the door open and hauled himself out, levelling his pistol across the roof at the little group who were now hurrying towards the farmhouse.

'Hold it right there!' he shouted.

There were six of them. Stone recognized Farnaby and the boy being hustled along by Zahran, still in his chauffeur's uniform. Two of the others turned at his shout and he saw that they were both armed, one with a revolver, the other with a machine-pistol. Bullets ripped and ricocheted along the roof of the Jag as Stone ducked. He leaned round the tail of the car and took a snap shot at the man with the revolver and saw him twist away and fall to his knees. The other one dived for shelter behind a heap of old tractor tyres but, as he drew back into the shelter of the car, Stone saw the two men who had tried to intercept them on the way in heading down the runway in a Land-Rover. He remembered Leo, still helpless in the front seat, virtually unprotected from their assailants' fire. As a last desperate hope he tugged his personal radio out of his pocket and gave his call sign.

'Delta Two, this is Delta One. Come in please!'

There was no answer. He tried again, but Nick was clearly out of range. The Land-Rover skidded to a halt a short distance away, one of the men in it covering Stone with the shotgun. Peering round the tail of the Jag he saw the other one emerging from the shelter of the tyres, the machine-pistol trained on the car. Reluctantly he threw his gun out onto the grass and stood up, raising his hands above his head.

They searched him quickly and efficiently and then the two men from the Land-Rover held him with his arms twisted behind his back while the third turned his attention to Leo.

'Be careful. She may be injured!' Stone said sharply but the man ignored him. He undid the seat-belt and dragged Leo out of the car onto the grass. She regained consciousness at this point, moaned and tried to sit up. He pushed her brutally back onto the ground and searched her, but, as usual, she was unarmed and carried no identification. When he was satisfied of this he dragged her to her feet and half marched, half carried, her towards the house. Stone and his two captors followed.

The rest of the group were in a big room at the back of the house which was obviously the farm kitchen. The PM's son was sitting at the table, ashen-faced, with Zahran behind him holding a pistol. At the end of the table was Farnaby, looking almost as shaken as the boy. As Stone was pushed through the door he was saying, his voice as always in moments of stress several notes higher than its normal pitch,

'You told me there was no risk! You never mentioned kidnapping…'

'Shut up!' said Zahran harshly. 'You're in this as deep as the rest of us.'

Farnaby turned to look at the new arrivals and his rather too fleshy mouth dropped open. 'Leonora! What on earth…'

Zahran, meanwhile, had recognized Stone.

'You!' he said, coming round the table. 'I thought I told them to finish you that night by the river.'

'It appears your men aren't as efficient as you thought,' Stone replied insolently.

'And you…' Zahran turned to Leo. 'Of course, the woman in the car-park.'

'But there's some mistake,' Farnaby babbled. 'This is Leonora Carr—the film star. You must recognize her!'

'So!' Zahran nodded. 'I thought the face was familiar.' He turned to Farnaby. 'You fool! You have been taken in by one of their agents. This man works for the Special Security Service—and the woman is obviously working with him.'

'But that's ridiculous!' protested Farnaby. 'I've known her for months. Everybody knows who she is…'

He broke off and stared at Leo in horrified comprehension. Zahran turned to his companions.

'Well, we know who they are, and we must assume that they have told their superiors where we are. The question now is what to do next.' He looked towards a man whom Stone had not noticed before. From his dress one would have taken him for an English gentleman farmer; only his dark complexion and hawk-like features proclaimed his origin to be quite other than that. Zahran spoke to him in a language which Stone took to be Arabic and he replied. The discussion continued for some little time, with occasional interjections from the others. There appeared to be some difference of opinion between Zahran and the man whom Stone took to be the owner of the farm but in the end Zahran seemed to have won the argument. Stone looked at Leo but she stood limply in her captor's grip, her head bent and her eyes downcast. He wondered if she was understanding any of what was being said. At the table Farnaby lit a cigarette with shaking hands and sat slumped as if overcome with shock. The young man stared from one face to another as if desperately trying to make sense of the situation. Stone caught his eye and tried to send a message of encouragement but he simply stared as if incapable of distinguishing friends from enemies.

Zahran turned to the men holding Stone and Leo and gave them an order of some kind. The owner of the house opened a door into the hallway and they were propelled through it and then through a further door which led to a steep flight of steps down into what was obviously a cellar. At the top of the steps the man unhooked a coil of rope from a nail and handed it to one of their guards. Stone submitted without wasting energy on resistance while his arms were bound tightly at the wrists and elbows behind his back. He was glad to see that Leo's hands were tied only at the wrists. Once they were satisfied with their work the men shoved them down the steps. Stone almost lost his balance and was saved only by the fact that his guards still had hold of him. Leo was not so fortunate. Half-way down the man holding her gave her a push and let her go. She stumbled and, unable to save herself, fell heavily down the rest of the flight and lay in a heap at the bottom. Above them a heavy door slammed to and Stone heard the bolts being shot home.

He dropped awkwardly onto his knees beside Leo and, unable to touch her with his hands, leaned down and put his face against her hair.

'Leo, are you all right?'

She made a small sound which was suspiciously like a sob and then struggled to her knees.

'I've heard some bloody stupid questions in my time, but that…' She looked at him, sniffed and managed a laugh. He looked back at her, in the dim light of the single, dust-furred electric bulb above their heads. The elegant white trouser suit was torn and filthy, her face was bruised and smudged with dirt and the sophisticated wig which was part of her Leonora Carr persona and which had miraculously survived the car crash had finally parted company with her head as she fell down the steps, leaving her own short curls flattened to her head and, in one place, matted with drying blood. On an impulse he leaned forward and kissed her cheek.

'OK?'

She let her head droop onto his shoulder for a moment.

'I shall be, in a minute.'

'Listen,' he said, 'could you understand any of what they were saying up there?'

She nodded and sat back on her heels. He could see her making an effort to clear her brain.

'Yes. They were arguing about what to do next. They think that we must have let Control know where they are.'

'Yes, I gathered that much.'

'The man who seems to own the house was trying to persuade Zahran to make a run for it. I think he didn't reckon on becoming actually involved in what's going on and he just wants to get rid of them. He suggested they take the Rolls and try to make it to Farnaby's place and then get a boat. Zahran thinks there will be road-blocks all round by now and they have a better chance of holding out here. He said, "What we are planning to do can still be done, from here".'

'What exactly are they planning, that's the question,' Stone murmured.

'Obviously they intended to get the PM's boy out of the country and then, presumably, to use his life as a bargaining counter. Now, they're going to do it from here.'

'They can't really expect to hold out here for more than a few hours, surely,' Stone said.

'It's a classic hostage situation, isn't it?' she replied. 'They've got him—and they've got us.' 'You know what that makes us, don't you?' he said flatly and she nodded. 'Pawns—very useful, but expendable.'

They were both silent for a moment. Leo shifted her position and winced. Stone looked around the cellar. A few feet away there was a dark heap of some kind, covered with a tarpaulin. There was no window or hatch which might have communicated with outside. He struggled to his feet and made a tour of inspection, finding it surprisingly difficult to keep his balance with his arms tied behind him. There was no way out except by the door through which they had come in. Finally he investigated the heap under the tarpaulin. He could not tell what it consisted of, but it was something firm but yielding, like bales of straw or sacks of grain. He went back to Leo.

'Come over here. We can lean against this. It'll be more

comfortable.'

She got to her feet and stumbled after him and they both flopped down against the tarpaulin. With something to lean against the discomfort of their pinioned arms was temporarily lessened. They sat close together, their shoulders touching. Leo looked at him.

'Well, what now?'

'Now we wait for Nick and Pascoe to do their stuff,' he responded, with more optimism than he felt.

'It could be a long wait,' she commented. 'We could be anywhere, for all they know.'

'That copper in the Sierra must have reported in when the horse-box cut him off,' Stone pointed out. 'That, and the fact that they haven't heard from us, will have alerted them to the fact that something's gone wrong. And don't forget the chopper. They should be able to get a good idea of the general area from the last reports and there's your car and the Rolls standing out there, plus a rather bent aeroplane. He can hardly miss that lot.'

'They're hardly likely to leave them standing out there, are they?' Leo pointed out. 'There's plenty of room in those barns to hide a fleet of cars.'

'It'll take time to get them all out of sight, though,' he said. 'The chopper may spot them first.'

'He may,' Leo said, and left it at that.

He leaned sideways and rubbed his cheek against her hair. Then he said suddenly,

'Why the hell are we sitting here like this, doing nothing? Twist round so that I can get at those ropes and see if I can undo them.'

They wriggled round so that they were back to back and after some manoeuvring Stone managed to get his fingertips on the knots at Leo's wrists; but with his arms fastened tightly at the elbows as well he was rapidly losing all feeling in his hands and the knots were tight.

'This could take some time,' he muttered.

'This is where we pay the price for clean living,' Leo remarked.

'What do you mean?'

'Well, if either of us smoked we might have a lighter. Then we could have burned through the ropes.

'You've been watching too much TV,' he told her. 'You don't think they'd have left us a lighter, if we had one, do you?'

He worked away for a while in silence. Then she said,

'Stone, you remember those long stories we were always going to tell one another—when we knew each other well enough?'

'Yes?'

'Well, perhaps this is the right moment. What do you think?'

He moved his fingers down and pressed hers, which were very cold.

'Yeah, why not?'

'OK,' she said. 'So, you were in the RAF. Pilot?'

'Of course.'

'Fighters? No, don't tell me—naturally. So what made you leave?'

He considered. 'Partly because a fighter pilot's active life isn't a very long one, and I didn't fancy a desk job. Partly because I got fed up with having to say "sir" to anyone who had more gold braid on his sleeve than I did. And partly…'

'Partly...?'

'Because to be a pilot in the RAF you have to be "an officer and a gentleman". They succeeded in making the first out of me but they never quite managed the second bit.'

'Really?' she sounded amused. 'Why was that?'

He was silent for a moment, working away at the knots. Then he said,

'I suppose because when you grew up in a children's home in Birkenhead you never feel quite at ease passing the port in the officers' mess.'

'A children's home?' she repeated softly. 'Why, Stone?'

A pause. Then, 'If you ever hear anyone calling me a right bastard, don't contradict them. Technically they're being completely accurate.'

This time she felt for his fingers and squeezed them. After a moment she said,

'But why weren't you adopted? There's usually plenty of

people only too anxious…'

Ah, well,' he said. 'My mum was all set to keep me, wasn't she. And she did, until she decided to get married—to a different feller. I was about 3 at the time. He didn't fancy having another bloke's kid around. When I was 4 the local authority took me away and put me in a children's home—for my own safety.'

There was a long silence. He gave up scrabbling at the rope.

'It's no good, I'm not getting anywhere with this. I can't feel my fingers any more.'

'Let me try yours,' she suggested, her voice unusually husky.

They rearranged their positions and he felt her icy fingers on his wrists. She said,

'And you stayed there—in the home?'

'Oh, I was fostered three times. It never worked.'

'Why not?'

'Not their fault. I just couldn't forgive them for not being my proper family. I either made myself such a pest that they gave up and took me back to the home or I ran away. The last time I was 12.1 spent a month living rough on the docks in Liverpool before they found me.'

'And yet you managed to end up as an officer in the RAF?'

'I was lucky. I had a good brain, and in those days education was still selective in that area. Getting into the grammar school did more for me than any foster family. And there were two masters at the school; one of them turned me from a playground thug into the school expert on the martial arts, the other one taught me maths. There's a wonderful stability about figures. No matter what happens, or what you're feeling like, two and two will still make four—and mathematical problems always have a solution, if you work at them long enough. When I left school I had to leave the home, too. That's the way it goes. One of the services seemed the obvious solution—a job, a place to live and a kind of substitute family. I fancied flying, so I picked the RAF; went in at the bottom and worked my way up. The day I got my wings was about the best day of my life—except for one thing.'

'What was that?'

'All the other blokes had their families there—doting mums, proud dads, girl-friends…'

'I should have thought you could have mustered three or four girl-friends,' she commented.

He grinned briefly. 'Yeah, well, that was the problem. There were three or four; but not one special one. And I couldn't very well ask them all, could I?'

She tugged at the rope around his wrists and gave a small groan of frustration.

'This is hopeless! I can't shift it. Hang on, let me have a try with my teeth.'

She twisted over and after a moment he felt her cheek against his hand and her teeth tugging at the rope. After a moment she mumbled,

'What did you do after you left the RAF?'

'Worked for anyone who'd pay me to fly a plane. Preferably somewhere I'd never been to before, somewhere where there was something exciting happening. I ended up flying for the guerrillas in El Salvador. Then I helped one of our people to get out of the country when the secret police were on his trail. I came back to London for a spot of leave and recognized a guy who'd been a top man in their secret police posing as a respectable business man. It turned out he was there to assassinate a prominent dissident who'd been given asylum and was getting his government a lot of bad publicity. I went to the authorities and they passed me on to Pascoe. I helped him nail the bloke and he offered me a permanent job.'

'No planes in Triple S,' Leo said indistinctly.

'No,' he agreed, 'But I'd got the flying bug out of my system by then. That was…'

'Nearly three years ago,' she supplied.

'You've been asking questions,' he accused her.

'Of course,' she replied. 'About Nick, as well as you.'

'How much did Pascoe tell you?'

'Just about as much as he told you about me, I should imagine,' she said. 'Which was the length of time you'd been with Triple S. Anything before that is a closed book, to everyone but him.'

Stone remembered the scene in Pascoe's office and said nothing. Leo sat up.

'I've got to take a break. My jaw aches and the taste of that rope makes me want to throw up.'

'Let me try again,' he suggested.

'No,' she said. 'Don't move. I've loosened it a bit, but if you start wriggling about it'll tighten up again. Just hang on a minute.'

Stone drew up his knees and leaned forward with his head on them, trying to get some relief from the cramping pains which were spreading down his back. He heard Leo turn away and spit onto the floor.

'God! I think they've used that rope for stringing up dead pigs or something!'

'Your turn,' he said. 'I've finished my story.' Then he remembered how Pascoe had warned them against asking questions that might bring back memories of her time at Oxford. 'Why did you give up acting?' he added.

'Do you mean why did I leave the RSC, or why did I give it all up when I left Hollywood?'

'Well, let's take the first one first. Why did you leave the Royal Shakespeare Company— that is it, isn't it?'

'You're learning. Oh, it was a personal thing. Some people would say trivial, except that people's lives aren't trivial. There was a man in the company—he's quite well known now, so I won't tell you his name. He fell in love with me, or thought he had. Unfortunately he was already married. His wife was an actress too—a very poor one. She was a helpless, neurotic creature who depended on him like a little child. When she found out about him and me she threatened to kill herself if he didn't stop seeing me. She'd already tried to commit suicide once before when she thought he was going to leave her. I was terrified she might succeed next time and I couldn't bear the thought of having another—of having somebody's death on my conscience. The only way for us to stop seeing each other was for one of us to leave the company, so when the film offer came along it seemed like a heaven-sent opportunity.'

'But it must have seemed unfair,' he said. 'I mean, I'm not

really into theatre but from what I’ve heard you were all set to be one of the great actresses of your generation.’

‘You don’t want to believe all you hear,’ she said drily. ‘I was good, but not that good. I was just very lucky. I went into the company at a time when good young actresses were a bit thin on the ground and I got the chance to play two superb parts which happened to suit me perfectly. I played Viola and I played Rosalind. I had a brilliant director to work with, they were two superb productions and I made my name. But I doubt if it would have gone on. I don’t think I’d have stayed in the theatre, whatever happened.’

‘Why not?’ he asked.

‘Actors are cannibals, you know,’ she replied. ‘They live off each other. And the audience lives off them. It’s like being eaten alive. I couldn’t have stood it for long.’

‘Is that why you dropped out after the film?’

‘Yes, more or less.’

‘It can’t have been easy though. I mean, you had it made—money, fame, all that.’

All that,’ she repeated ironically. ‘Yes, the backbiting and the scandal and the letters from men threatening to kill themselves if you don’t make a date with them, and their wives threatening to kill you if you do! Not to mention the crazy journalists making up stories about you to fit their editor’s requirements. That was when I first started to disguise myself. I had my hair cut short and a wig made to look like it used to be. That way I could think of Leonora Carr and myself as two different people. Then one day I woke up and said, “What the hell am I doing here?” So I packed a bag and drove to the airport and got on a plane for Athens.’

‘Why Athens?’

She was silent for a moment. Then she said,

‘I once spent some time there before when I was feeling pretty low and it helped me. Some people head for the sea when they need spiritual comfort, some head for the desert or the mountains. I go to Greece.’

‘So how did you end up working for Triple S?’ he asked.

‘While I was in Greece I posed as an author doing research

for a book. I met quite a lot of people, including a shipping man—a kind of minor Onassis. After a bit I began to suspect that he was making most of his money from running guns for the PLO and the IRA. The idea of him sitting in his villa on Aegina on the proceeds of people being blown up in Beirut and Belfast made me very angry, so I set about getting some proof. When he came to London on a business trip I followed. I knew James Pascoe slightly—his niece was at school with me—so I went to him and told him what I knew. The man was arrested and convicted...'

'Of course, the Aristarchos case!' Stone exclaimed.

'That's the one. After that Pascoe had the idea of setting up the Cavendish Agency. He suggested it to me and I thought it sounded as if—well, as if I might at least be doing something useful. So there it is—and here we are.'

'Yes, indeed,' he agreed soberly. Then he added suddenly, 'Leo, we're crazy. There are two lots of ropes round my arms. It's pointless you trying to untie me. Turn round and let me see if I can get my teeth into your rope.'

Chapter 10

In the van, parked now in the clearing below the tower on Leith Hill, Nick was searching the airwaves for some word from either Stone or Leo.

'Nothing!' he muttered. 'Not a dicky-bird!'

A phone buzzed and Mitch, Triple S's chief communications expert, picked it up.

'Pascoe, for you on the scrambler,' he said, handing it over.

'Delta Two,' said Nick into the phone.

'Any news?' Pascoe asked.

'Nothing so far,' Nick replied. 'How are things at your end?'

'Not good,' said Pascoe. 'I've informed the PM. We have a direct line to the private office at Number 10, and not surprisingly they're expecting some results pretty damn soon. We've set up road-blocks on all roads within a ten-mile radius of the position where that police car was stopped by the horse-box. And guess what—the owner of the horse-box turns out to be an Iranian business man who has an Arab horse-breeding stud there.'

'Have you checked his place out?' Nick asked.

'The local police are doing that now, but I don't anticipate any positive results. After all, they led us right to it.'

'You reckon they went that way just so that he could cut off anyone who happened to be following?'

'That's my interpretation. But it doesn't tell us where they were aiming for eventually. If we don't hear anything from the road-blocks within the next half-hour we shall have to assume they've gone to ground somewhere within the ten-mile radius. Any word from the chopper?'

'He says he's pretty sure that the Rolls isn't moving along any of the roads in the area to the south of the Downs. No sign of Omega's Jag, either.'

'Where the devil have those two got to?' Pascoe demanded. 'No reports from the police of any crashes?'

'No, sir. We've checked. They just seem to have disappeared off the face of the earth at the moment.'

'Well, tell the chopper to keep searching as long as he can

and keep me informed. That's all for now.'

Mitch had been speaking on the radio while Nick talked to Pascoe. Now he said,

'Message from the local nick. A farmer has just phoned in to report a quote "female maniac in a white Jaguar" unquote who almost collided with him head on in one of the lanes near here. He took the registration number— that is one of ours, isn't it?'

Nick looked at the number which Mitch had written down.

'Yes, that's the one we're looking for. Where exactly did this happen?'

Mitch consulted the ordnance survey map and laid his finger on a spot.

'There.'

'And there is the place where the police car lost contact with the Rolls,' said Nick. 'Just around the corner. Obviously they were trying to bypass the obstruction and pick the Rolls up further on.'

'According to the farmer they were going at about seventy miles an hour along a single-track road,' Mitch remarked.

'Well, they'd need to, wouldn't they,' Nick returned, 'to make up the difference.'

'Who is this "female maniac" anyway?' Mitch wanted to know. 'Doesn't sound like Stone, letting a woman drive—specially on an outing like that.'

'He probably didn't have much option,' Nick said. 'She's a very strong-minded lady. Now look, suppose they did pick up the Rolls again—if it stuck to that road they must have been going down onto the lower ground. Mitch, if you'd kidnapped the PM's son where would you head for?'

'Out of the country—fast,' Mitch replied.

'Which means either one of the channel ports, or a plane,' said Nick. 'Is there an airstrip anywhere near here?'

'Well, if you open that door and hold your hand out with a bun in it you can practically feed the airplanes on their way in to Gatwick,' Mitch remarked.

'Gatwick!' Nick leaned over the map. 'Yes, of course. But surely they wouldn't have the nerve to head for a public airport. Anyway, they won't get far if they have. The first thing Pascoe did was to put a call out to all airports, ferries and so on. No, I mean small private airfields.'

'Well, there are several along the south coast; or there's Biggin Hill to the east.'

'Outside the ten-mile limit.' Nick said. 'They'd have been stopped at one of the police check-points. It's got to be somewhere local. Listen, put a call through to air traffic control at Gatwick. See if they've logged any movements by small aircraft in this area.'

'Right,' said Mitch.

Nick opened the door of the van and stepped down onto the short turf of the clearing. Ahead of him the ground sloped away so steeply that he was looking over the tops of the oak and beech trees which clung to the escarpment. Beyond them lay the undulating farmland which stretched away to the distant, hazy whale-back humps of the South Downs; an ordered geometry of fields and woods dotted with villages and farms and crossed with roads, along which moving vehicles sent back sharp glints of reflected light from the westering sun. Somewhere, Nick thought, in that supremely civilized landscape, Stratos Zahran was holed up like a predatory animal with his prisoner—or prisoners. With every minute that passed Nick was becoming more certain that Stone and Leo must have been captured, or worse. If either of them was still free they would undoubtedly have found their way to a telephone by now and made contact. Nick bent his mind to the landscape in front of him as if some subtle antennae in his brain could pick up a signal which could not be transmitted by more conventional means.

To his left he could just make out the complex of buildings and runways which made up Gatwick airport, with a big jet slanting in well below the height at which he was standing. Immediately in front of him the land was not so flat, but somewhere in those gentle folds there must be a field large enough for an aircraft to take off. He turned back and climbed into the van.

'Gatwick traffic control report no known movements of light aircraft in this area in the last two hours,' Mitch said.

'Well, maybe they're still down there, somewhere,' Nick said, 'waiting to take off. Waiting for dark perhaps. Listen, get onto the local nick again and see if they can tell you whether any of the farmers around here use a light aircraft for crop-spraying or something. There must be some pretty big landowners in this part of the country and it's not unusual for them to use private planes. Oh, and while you're about it—just ask if any of the farms round here have been sold in the last year or so to Middle Eastern purchasers, or any foreign nationals for that matter.'

While Mitch went to work on that Nick picked up the mike and called the helicopter.

'Firebird, this is Watchdog.'

'Receiving you, Watchdog.'

'Still no sign of either the Rolls or the Jag?'

'Negative, Watchdog.'

'OK. Here's a new tack. Can you take a look at some of the farms and other large buildings down there and see if there is any sign of an airstrip, or anywhere an aircraft could take off?'

'Roger, Watchdog,' responded the pilot, 'but it'll have to be a quick look. Ten more minutes and I've got to push off to refuel.'

'OK, Firebird,' Nick replied. 'I'll see if I can organize a replacement for you. Let me know if you spot anything. Out.'

He made the necessary calls to arrange for another helicopter to take over. Just as he finished Mitch said,

'Pascoe for you again.'

Nick took the phone.

'Delta Two.'

'The balloon's gone up,' Pascoe said. 'The PM's office had a call five minutes ago. They're threatening to kill the boy unless the government announces by eight o'clock tomorrow morning that they have withdrawn all objections to a representative of the PLO attending the conference.'

'Where did the call come from?' Nick asked.

'A phone-box in West London,' Pascoe replied. 'Obviously they must have had someone standing by to pass on the message.' 'Not a lot of help there,' Nick commented. 'What's the official attitude?'

'Officially,' said Pascoe, 'of course there's no question of yielding to terrorist demands. But as long as we can keep the lid on this there is still room for the government to manoeuvre. If it becomes public knowledge on the other hand they will have no choice but to take a hard line if they want to maintain any credibility.'

'Tricky,' commented Nick.

'It's a good deal more than that!' Pascoe said sharply. 'It's absolutely vital that no word of this should get out to the press before tomorrow morning. If you get the faintest hint of any reporters sniffing around, clobber them.'

'Right,' said Nick.

'Any further developments at your end?'

Nick told him what there was to tell.

'I'm on my way down,' Pascoe said. 'There's no more I can do here.'

Nick had been aware of Mitch talking on the radio and when he put the phone down Mitch put a sheet of paper in front of him.

'Bingo!' he said.

'What?' Nick asked.

'The local police have come up with an address. This place was sold a year back to a Mr Rashid, who claims to be from Kuwait.'

Nick looked at the address on the paper.

'Huntersford Farm. Where is it?'

'Here,' Mitch pointed to the map.

Nick reached for the microphone.

'Firebird, this is Watchdog. Come in please.'

'Firebird here.'

'Firebird, can you check a place called Huntersford Farm?' He gave the map coordinates. 'See if you can spot any sign of a light aircraft or possibly the two cars we're looking for.'

'Roger Watchdog. Firebird out.'

Nick went outside again. He could see the chopper beating away to the south-west. He lifted his binoculars and searched the ground in the same direction but it was impossible to pick out the farm at this distance. He saw the chopper swing round and then drop lower. Mitch called him from inside the van.

'Watchdog, this is Firebird.' The pilot's voice came flatly from the loudspeaker. 'I think this may be what you're looking for. There is definitely an airstrip here. It's only grass and I nearly missed it but there's a windsock flying by the corner of a barn. No sign of an aircraft, or of the cars, but there would be plenty of room in the barns to hide them.'

'Thank you Firebird,' Nick said. 'We'll take it from here.'

'OK, Watchdog. I'm off home to bye-byes. Oh, by the way, I don't know if it's any help, but there are a couple of bloody great skid marks down there on the runway. Looks like two vehicles of some kind nearly had a head-on collision.'

'Very interesting,' murmured Nick, '—but I don't know what it means. Thanks for your help, Firebird. Out.'

He called Pascoe on the scrambler phone in his car and told him the news.

'Don't do anything until I get to you,' Pascoe said. 'I'll rendezvous with you at...' he gave a set of co-ordinates which identified a road junction about half a mile from the farm, '...in forty-five minutes. I will inform all other units. You just get down there and keep an eye on the place from a distance. Is that understood?'

'Understood,' Nick replied.

'Marriot!' Pascoe's voice had a warning edge. 'It's obviously possible that Zahran may be holding Delta One and Omega. I don't want any knight-errantry from you. Right?'

'Right,' said Nick heavily.

As they bumped away down the track which led to the road, the sun had set, leaving a banner of purple and crimson cloud above the western horizon; and the shadows deepened as they wound down off the hills. By the time they reached the rendezvous the long summer evening was almost over and when Pascoe joined them it was dark. He brought with him the two agents codenamed Kappa One and Two, Barney Lightfoot and 'Viv' Vivian, and a police car containing two of the top brass from the local force. Ten minutes later they were joined by an army staff car and a truck full of quiet men in dark clothing who wore no insignia or badges of rank. Pascoe conferred with the other officers and then called Nick over.

'How sure are we that this is the place?' one of them asked.

'Not sure at all, sir,' Nick replied. 'We only know that it belongs to a man of Middle Eastern origin who apparently has a private plane; and we assume that as none of our road-blocks have picked up Zahran and the rest of them they must still be somewhere in this area.'

'Unless the birds have flown, literally,' said another man.

'That is possible,' Pascoe conceded, 'but there are no records of light aircraft movements in this area for the relevant time.'

'Well,' said the army officer, 'this is your show, Pascoe. What do we do next?'

'I shall pay a call on Mr Rashid,' said Pascoe. 'After all, he may be a perfectly law-abiding citizen. Marriot, you can come with me.'

Nick got into the driving seat of Pascoe's car and they drove slowly up the lane and turned into the drive which led to the farm. The front of the house was dark. Nick wondered what would happen if they rang the doorbell and got no reply. His speculations were interrupted by the sudden chatter of a machine-pistol and a line of bullets kicked up the gravel just ahead of the car. Nick stood on the brake and the car skidded to a halt. A voice shouted to them from an upstairs window.

'That's far enough! Identify yourself.'

Pascoe wound down his window.

'Commander James Pascoe of the Special Security Service. And you, I assume, are Stratos Zahran.'

'Who I am is of no importance,' came the answer. 'What I have to say to you is. You know that we have a prisoner who is very important to your Prime Minister. We have also two of your agents—the man Stone and a girl who calls herself Leonora Carr. We have given your government until eight o'clock tomorrow morning to make the public announcement that they will accept the representative of the PLO at the Geneva conference; but now that you have found us I am tightening the deadline. Unless I have a personal assurance from your Prime Minister that our request will be met by midnight we shall shoot one of your agents. That will perhaps convince you that we mean business. You have one hour and a half, Mr Pascoe. That is all.'

'That's ridiculous!' Pascoe exclaimed. 'How can we possibly get a decision like that through in that time?'

'That, Mr Pascoe,' Zahran replied, 'is, as you say, your problem. I need not point out, of course, that the slightest sign of any military or police activity in the vicinity of the house will result in the immediate deaths of both your agents. Now go back and deliver your message, before I shoot your driver!'

'Let's go,' Pascoe said quietly.

Nick put the car into reverse and backed away slowly down the drive, then turned and drove back to the junction where the others were waiting. Pascoe went to report to his fellow officers and Nick joined Mitch, Barney and Viv by the communications van.

'Well?' Mitch asked.

'It's them all right,' Nick said.

'We guessed that when we heard the shots,' commented Viv. 'Either that—or they've got a very nasty way with trespassers down here.'

'What about Stone and this Omega character?' Barney asked.

'They've got them too,' Nick told him. There was a kind of leaden chill in his stomach. 'They're threatening to shoot one of them if they don't get a personal undertaking from the PM by midnight.'

'Midnight!' said Viv, and Barney murmured softly, 'Christ!'

Mitch silently offered Nick a hip-flask but he shook his head. Tonight, of all nights, he needed his brain as clear and quick as he could make it. They were all quiet for a while. Mitch and the other two knew and respected the long-standing partnership between Nick and Stone and understood what was going through his mind—or thought they did.

'Who is Omega?' Barney said again, after a while. 'I've never heard of the guy.'

'It's not a guy, it's a girl,' Nick said unwillingly.

'A girl!' said Viv, and they all looked at Nick with new speculation in their eyes.

Pascoe came over.

'We must know what's going on in there,' he said. 'I want

someone to plant listening devices near any window where there seems to be activity; but remember, if they catch a glimpse of you it could mean one or both of our people being shot. Zahran has a reputation for sticking to his word in an utterly ruthless manner.'

'We'll go,' said Barney at once.

'No!' said Nick. 'This one's down to me— and I'll do it on my own. Two people means twice the chance of being spotted.'

'Very well,' Pascoe agreed. 'Keep in touch by radio, and try to find out where the hostages are being held. Good luck.'

Nick went into the van and collected the equipment he needed. Then he smeared his face with camouflage make-up, checked his gun and tucked a couple of spare clips into his pocket.

'Do you want me to run you up as far as the entrance?' Barney offered.

Nick shook his head. 'No, on a still night like this they'd hear the car as soon as we started the engine. I'm going cross-country, on foot.'

He took a last look at the map, hung a pair of night-glasses round his neck and headed for a gate leading into a nearby field. Once over the gate he turned to his right and slunk along the bottom of a hedgerow like a fox on a nocturnal hunting expedition. It seemed to take a very long time to traverse the three fields which separated him from the farm, stopping every fifty yards or so to strain his eyes and ears into the darkness for any sign of someone on watch; but at last he found himself among the barns at the rear of the house. From here on he moved even more cautiously, checking every building before he passed it, until he came to the last of a straggling series of outbuildings, which appeared to be a woodshed. From here only a lawned garden area separated him from the house itself. There were lights in the windows of a room on the ground floor but the windows themselves appeared to be covered with shutters or blinds. Nick crouched in the shadow of the shed and studied the house and the space between it and himself. To his left a long wall ran the length of the garden and in the corner where it met the house there appeared to be a gate. Nick turned and worked his way back round the woodshed and across a small yard until he reached the far side of the wall. Sheltered by it from the view of anyone in the house he glided silently along it to the gate. A gentle pressure on the latch revealed the fact that it was locked. He looked up. Along the top of the wall there was some kind of creeper, sufficient to give a bit of cover. He reached up, got his fingers over the top of the brickwork and heaved himself up, scrabbling with his toes for crevices which would give him a purchase, until he was able to lie flat along the top of the wall. It was then that he realized that the sheltering creeper was a berberis, every branch of which was covered with needle-sharp thorns.

It took him several long, painful minutes to free himself from the grip of the branches, which clung like claws to his flesh. Then he lay still and inspected the house again. The upper windows were all dark but he was certain that there must be watchers in them, as there had been at the front of the house. How many men did Zahran have with him? There was Farnaby, of course, but Nick reckoned that he might be more a hindrance than a help to the terrorists in the present situation. Apart from that there was the man who had met Zahran when he arrived; the owner of the farm, presumably, and any men he happened to have working for him. Quite possibly there were no more than five or six of them. One at the front of the house, a couple at least to guard the hostages, Zahran himself—maybe only one watching the back. Nick wished he could be sure of that.

As he watched his eye caught a faint, metallic glint in the central window of the upper storey. He lifted the glasses to his eyes. Yes, there it was—the faint reflection of light from below on the barrel of a rifle. He searched the other windows but as far as he could tell they were empty. The man holding the gun was not visible, standing back a little presumably from the window itself. Nick eased himself along the wall to the corner. As long as he kept close to the house the man would not be able to see him unless he leaned out. In the corner was a small shrubbery. Nick swung his legs over the edge of the wall and let himself down among the bushes, suppressing a yelp of pain as the sharp thorns of the berberis found a gap between his jacket and the top of his trousers and clawed a weal across his stomach.

For a few minutes he crouched in the darkness among the bushes. There was no sign of movement in the garden. Stooping low he began to creep along the back of the house towards the lighted windows. When he reached the first of them he could hear a low murmur of voices from inside—two, no three voices; then, unmistakably, Farnaby's high-pitched, protesting tones. Nick reached up and pressed the suction pad on the first listening device to the glass of the window. Then he slunk along to the second window and fixed another one there. Once satisfied that both were firmly attached he crept back to the shrubbery in the corner and worked his way in among the bushes. Securely hidden and far enough away from the upper window where the guard was posted he felt safe in using his radio.

'Control—' he spoke scarcely above a whisper, '—this is Delta Two.'

Pascoe himself answered.

'This is Control. Well done, Delta Two. We have excellent reception. What have you to report?'

'One man with a rifle in the central first floor window at the back,' Nick murmured. 'The rest seem to be in one room on the ground floor, also at the back. I think I heard three of them. Can you tell if the hostages are there?'

'We think the main hostage is with them,' Pascoe replied, 'but there is no sign at the moment that Delta One and Omega are there.'

'Do you want me to try and locate them?' Nick asked.

'Negative, Delta Two,' came the instant response. 'We can't take any further risks. You can come back now.

'Negative, Control,' replied Nick in his turn. 'I'm staying here. At least I'm close enough to do something in an emergency.'

There was a slight hesitation before Pascoe responded.

'Very well, stay if you are quite sure that there is no risk of your being seen. But you are to take no action without prior instructions. Is that clear?'

'Clear, Control,' Nick said grudgingly. 'Delta Two out.'

* * *

Back in the communications van Pascoe and the other officers bent over their maps while Mitch, who had been joined by an Arab speaking interpreter from the Triple S staff, monitored the conversation going on in the farmhouse.

'Well, there it is,' said Pascoe. 'No possibility of action by the Government before midnight.'

'Do you reckon this man Zahran will stick to his deadline?' asked the colonel in charge of the SAS contingent.

'Almost certainly,' Pascoe replied grimly.

'Haven't got a lot of choice then, have we,' the other man concluded.

Mitch turned away from his radio console.

'He's just sent someone to fetch our two, sir.'

Pascoe straightened up. 'Right. We're agreed then. I'll get up to the house and try to keep them talking.'

* * *

It had taken Stone almost half an hour to free Leo and it was some time after that before her numbed fingers could work loose the knots which bound his arms. By the time she succeeded he was sweating with the pain in his cramped shoulders and back. She knelt behind him kneading the knotted muscles while he rubbed his wrists until at last the blood began to circulate again. Then he rolled up the pieces of rope and tucked them out of sight.

'OK,' he said, 'when they come to get us they must think we're still tied up. Pretend to be unconscious, or unable to get up anyway. I want whoever comes to have to get close. When they do we'll take them. Right?'

'Right,' she confirmed.

They were silent for a moment.

'I wonder what's going on out there,' Stone murmured.

Leo shrugged. 'I imagine Pascoe has realized that Zahran is still somewhere in the area, and that we're either dead or prisoners. God only knows how long it'll take them to track us down to this particular farm. I wonder if Zahran has given them a deadline yet.'

'He won't want to hang about, that's for sure,' Stone replied. 'He must know it's only a matter of time before he's found.'

'You know the thought that frightens me most?' said Leo. 'The idea that he might make a run for it and leave us down here.'

'It wouldn't be for long,' he reassured her. 'Nick's out there somewhere. He's got a nose like a bloodhound and he won't rest till he's found us.'

She turned and smiled at him. 'No, I know he won't.'

He looked at her. The elegant white suit was very little protection against the chill of the cellar. She sat with her knees drawn up to her chin but he saw that she was shivering. He put his arm round her and drew her close and they settled down together to wait, like a couple of lost children. He glanced at his watch. It was coming up to ten o'clock.

The time passed slowly. They talked in snatches, about Pascoe and Triple S, about places they had visited, cases they had worked on. Every so often they forced themselves to get up and move around to keep themselves alert but it was lucky for them that, when the sound of the bolts being shot back finally came, they were sitting down, for they had less warning than they had anticipated. Instantly they both thrust their hands behind them and lay back against the tarpaulin.

'On your feet!' commanded one of Zahran's men.

Neither of them moved. The man came half-way down the steps, while a second stood at the top covering them with an automatic pistol.

'Come on, get up! You're wanted,' the first man repeated.

Stone looked at Leo. She was lying with her head slumped, her face half hidden against the tarpaulin.

'She can't get up,' he said. 'There's something wrong with her. I think she was injured when we crashed the car. She may be dead, for all I know.'

The man came to the bottom of the steps. He looked worried. Stone had guessed correctly that the idea that one of their valuable hostages might already be dead had got him jumpy. He came closer, peering at Leo. Stone willed the man at the top of the stairs to come down but he remained where he was, watching.

'You! Out of the way.' The first man gestured at him with his gun. Stone wriggled backwards, getting to his knees, pretending to have difficulty in rising. The Arab grabbed Leo by the hair and jerked her head back, but her eyes remained closed and she flopped back again as soon as he let her go. Stone mentally awarded her full marks for self-control. The man said something over his shoulder in Arabic and at last his companion holstered the automatic and ran down the stairs to help him. They bent over Leo, taking her by an arm each to drag her to her feet. At that instant Leo jerked her head forward and up, butting the first man hard on the bridge of the nose, and at the same time bringing up her knees to catch him sharply in the pit of the stomach. Simultaneously Stone brought the edge of his hand down on the back of the other man's neck. He crumpled without a sound, while the first staggered back to collapse groaning a few feet away. Stone caught Leo by the hand, dragging her to her feet, and they turned towards the door.

'Very good!' said Stratos Zahran. 'I must say that Triple S trains its people extremely well.'

He was standing in the doorway with the machine-pistol in his hands. Stone was filled with a wild desire to run straight at him and knock the mocking smile off his face, but he knew that one sudden move would almost certainly spell death for both of them.

'Up here!' said Zahran, sharply.

Slowly they climbed the stairs towards him. Behind them they could hear the two men beginning to recover and stagger to their feet. Zahran shouted over his shoulder,

'Nadim!'

The man who had greeted him when he came off the boat appeared and there was a short exchange between the two of them in their own language. Zahran indicated with a movement of the gun that Stone and Leo should pass him into the hallway.

'Tie them,' he said. 'And this time, make sure it's tight.'

Stone gritted his teeth as his arms were once again forced together in the small of his back and tied so that the rope bit into his flesh. He saw Leo wince as her arms too were twisted behind her but she submitted without resistance. The other men stumbled out through the cellar door and were subjected to a scathing harangue in Arabic before being dismissed to the kitchen and replaced by the two who had tried to stop the Jag when they first arrived. Zahran looked from Stone to Leo.

'So,' he said. 'Now we wait.'

The hall was large and square, almost a room in its own right. At one end was the front door and at the other, beyond the entrance to the kitchen, it narrowed to a passage, at the end of which was a window covered by a blind. In the centre of the square section was a polished oak table. Stone and Leo stood with their backs to the wall opposite the cellar door and the staircase leading to the upper floor. Zahran wandered over and stood in front of Leo, looking at her curiously.

'Leonora Carr!' he mused. 'So this is what happened to you. I saw that film, you know. There was a scene in which you and the man were in bed together. Tell me, what was really going on under those silk sheets?'

Leo looked back at him without expression. 'Nothing that would have been of any interest to you, from what I know of your reputation.'

Zahran bared his teeth, half a smile, half a snarl.

'Later in that scene you got out of bed. We saw you walk across to the window—naked.'

Leo continued to meet his eyes. 'As it happens,' she said evenly, 'that wasn't me. They filmed that later with another girl. I didn't even know the shot was there until I saw the finished film. But I don't expect you to believe that.'

Stone remembered the scene, vividly. He believed what Leo had said and found, somewhat to his surprise, that he was glad of it.

Zahran laughed. 'You're right, I don't believe it. You are a woman without shame. You deserve to be punished.'

He turned away and perched himself on the edge of the table watching them.

'You will be interested to hear, no doubt, that your colleagues have already located us.' Stone caught Leo's eye with something like triumph but her look remained impassive. 'Oh yes,' Zahran went on, 'I must give them credit. They have been extremely efficient. I have spoken with your commander, James Pascoe. Officially, your government has until eight o'clock tomorrow to accept our demands, but I have told him that unless we have an assurance by midnight that those demands will be met one of you will be shot, as a demonstration of our determination.' He looked at his watch. 'It is now eleven thirty. Of course, your government will not concede immediately. They will negotiate, play for time, try to wear us down—that is the technique, isn't it? It will undoubtedly be necessary to convince them that we mean what we say. So I think you can make up your minds that in half an hour one of you will be dead.'

A man's voice shouted something in Arabic from the landing above and Zahran turned and ran upstairs. A moment later, distorted by a loud-hailer but instantly recognizable, they heard Pascoe's voice.

'Zahran! This is Commander Pascoe. I want to talk to you.'

They heard Zahran answer but the words were muffled and indistinguishable. When Pascoe spoke again he had abandoned the loud-hailer and Stone found that however hard he strained his ears he could not make out what was being said. The conversation went on for what seemed like a very long time. Stone knew that Pascoe was doing exactly what Zahran had expected and playing for time. He could only hope and pray that his chief understood just how real the threat was; on the other hand he knew that if the price of a successful operation against men like these was his life, or Leo's, then the price would have to be paid.

The chatter of the machine-pistol from upstairs jerked them all to attention. For a second Stone met Leo's eyes and saw the same wild supposition as that which was in his own mind. Had Zahran shot Pascoe—and what would it mean for them if he had? Then they heard the sound of a car being reversed fast away from the house. Someone, at any rate, had survived to drive it. It occurred to Stone that Nick might very well have been with Pascoe.

Zahran came down the stairs, slowly, swinging the gun from one hand, like a man with a treat in store which he is putting off in order to savour the enjoyment longer.

'It is as I thought,' he said. 'Excuses—the difficulty of assembling Cabinet Ministers at this time of night et cetera; demands for proof that we actually hold you and that you are not already dead; questions about what we propose to do if our demands are met; offers of an aircraft to fly us out of the country if we hand over the hostages safely… Delaying tactics, all of it. So, it is necessary to prove that we intend to carry out our threats.' He paused, looking from Stone to Leo. The girl, I think. To the English, the death of a woman always comes as more of a shock.' He gestured to his two subordinates. Take him over there, out of the way.'

Before they could get hold of him Stone lunged forward, hoping to knock Zahran down with a body charge, but he swung round and smashed the butt of the gun into his face. The two men grabbed him as he staggered and Zahran hit him in the stomach for good measure. Then he raised the gun and levelled it at Leo.

'Not her, Zahran!' Stone choked, fighting for breath. 'Shoot me instead.'

Zahran cast him a mocking, sideways look.

'Such chivalry! Be patient, your turn will come.'

Stone gazed desperately at Leo. She was deathly pale but her eyes never left Zahran.

'You know your trouble, Stone,' she said, without looking at him. 'You've never been able to accept the equality of the sexes!'

Zahran braced the gun under his arm and took aim. He was about five feet from where Stone was being held, each of his captors tightly gripping an arm. Stone measured the distance with his eye and, as Zahran's finger tightened on the trigger, he threw his whole weight onto the men who were holding hire and, using them as a pivot, kicked out with both feet. He caught Zahran under the forearm just as the first bullet was fired. The gun jerked upwards and a line of bullets scored up the wall and across the ceiling; but Leo twisted forward and fell to her knees, blood staining the white suit.

Stone's impetus had dragged hire free from his captors' grip and, unable to save himself, he fell heavily on his back, knocking the breath from his body. Zahran, still holding the gun, swung round and aimed it at him but, as he did so, there was a crash of breaking glass from the window at the end of the passage and Nick hurtled through it, feet first. Zahran raised the gun to cover the new target but as he opened fire Nick threw himself flat and a single shot from his pistol took the terrorist in the stomach and hurled him back across the oak table. At the same time there were two or three heavy explosions as stun grenades went off in several of the rooms, followed by more breaking glass and splintering wood as the men of the SAS came in through windows all round the ground floor. Helpless and only half conscious Stone rolled himself out of the way against the wall and waited for the trampling feet and the occasional shots to cease. He saw Farnaby bundled out of the back kitchen and out through the front door, followed with an almost equal lack of ceremony by the Prime Minister's son. He looked round for Nick and saw him kneeling on the floor on the other side of the room, cradling Leo in his arms. Pascoe came swiftly through the front door and went straight to them. Stone staggered to his feet and was immediately seized by a hefty soldier.

'OK, sunshine, on your way!' He was shoved towards the door.

'Get off me, you moron!' he ground out between gritted teeth.

He was rescued by Barney Lightfoot who had come in with Pascoe.

'All right,' he said. 'He's one of ours.'

The soldier released his grip, somewhat reluctantly.

'Cut me loose, for God's sake,' Stone growled.

As soon as his arms were free he staggered over to where Nick and Pascoe were still huddled over Leo and dropped on his knees beside them. The left hand side of her shirt was completely soaked in blood and her eyes were closed. Pascoe was holding her wrist.

'Is she alive?' Stone mumbled, through lips that felt as numb as his arms.

At the moment,' Pascoe said.

Two men came in through the front door carrying a stretcher.

'Over here, quickly,' Pascoe called.

As they were about to lift her onto the stretcher Leo's eyelids flickered and opened. Her gaze went from Pascoe to Nick and finally rested hazily on Stone. The pale lips twitched in a faint effort at a smile.

'Precious…' she whispered. 'Definitely—a pearl of great price…'

They laid her on the stretcher and wrapped her in blankets, and the two bearers carried her out to the waiting ambulance. Someone called Pascoe and he straightened up and went over. Nick got up too but Stone stayed where he was on the floor. Suddenly he was aware of the blood trickling from his nose; of the pain in his back and stomach which blended into a single, sickening ache filling the whole of his body. He started to shiver.

Nick looked at him for the first time. He crouched down again beside him and put a fist under his chin to lift his head.

'You know,' he said, studying his face, 'If I didn't know you better, I'd say you'd been in a fight.'

'Get lost!' muttered Stone and found to his annoyance that his teeth were chattering.

Nick stripped off his jacket and put it round his shoulders.

'C'mon,' he said. 'We'd better get you down to the hospital and have you checked over.'

* * *

An hour later all three men were in a small hospital waiting-room. Stone, his face cleaned and patched up, was huddled in a blanket, his hands round a mug of hot tea. X-rays had shown no bones broken but the hospital had wanted to keep him in overnight just the same. He had refused—politely, but in no uncertain terms. Nick sat opposite him, his long legs thrust out in front of him, hands deep in the pockets of his jacket, resting his head against the wall behind him. By the window stood Pascoe, who had just joined them. Leo was in the operating theatre, and they were all waiting for news.

'I shall want a full report tomorrow, of course,' Pascoe was saying, 'but tell me briefly what happened.'

Stone told him.

'So Leo wasn't shot by accident in the fighting?' Pascoe said.

'No,' Stone said flatly. 'It was pure, coldblooded murder.'

'I can confirm that,' Nick said. 'I heard Zahran giving the orders. That's why I...'

'Why you went in before my signal and jeopardized the whole operation,' Pascoe said drily.

'I'd have been dead if he hadn't,' Stone told him.

They were silent for a moment, then Nick said,

'What was she talking about when she came round, just before they took her away?'

'No idea,' said Stone. 'Something about pearls...'

'Oh, surely she was referring to you,' said Pascoe, raising an eyebrow.

'Me?' he queried.

'A pun on your name? A precious Stone—a pearl of great price...?'

Stone stared at him for a moment, then he said, 'Oh,' and looked away and Nick was touched to see him blush.

The door opened and a man came in wearing a surgeon's gown.

'Commander Pascoe?'

Stone and Nick came to their feet simultaneously.

'Yes?' Pascoe said.

'You're waiting for news about Leonora Cavendish—the young woman with the gunshot wounds?'

'Yes!' said Pascoe again.

'Are you a relative?'

'No, I'm not. Get on with it, man!'

The surgeon looked at Stone and Nick.

'Are either of you related to the young lady?' They shook their heads dumbly. 'It's all rather irregular,' he continued. 'We usually only give information to the next of kin ...'

'Oh, for God's sake!' exclaimed Pascoe.

'Here!'

He thrust his warrant card under the man's nose. The surgeon took a step back.

'Oh, I see,' he said nervously.

'Well?' Pascoe snapped.

'It's early days yet, of course,' the surgeon began, trying to recover his dignity, 'but we think she should pull through. We removed two bullets, one from the apex of the lung and one from the shoulder. She's lost a lot of blood, of course, but provided there are no complications... Would you say she was a reasonable strong, healthy young woman?'

'Yes!' said three voices simultaneously.

'Well, in that case I'm fairly sure that she will be all right,' the surgeon concluded. 'Of course, if that first bullet had been an inch or two lower...'

Nick looked at Stone.

'That's down to you, mate,' he said quietly. 'I owe you one.'

'We both do,' Pascoe put in, unexpectedly.

Chapter 11

Stone whistled happily as he parked his car in the Chelsea square. It was a sultry August night and the air was heavy with dust and the smell of petrol fumes. Leo had returned the previous day from convalescence in Greece and her first action—he told himself it must have been her first action—had been to call him and invite him to dinner. He had been a little disappointed when she had turned down his suggestion that he should take what leave he had coming to him and go to Greece with her, on the grounds that he would soon get bored with the company of a semi-invalid who wanted to do nothing but lie in the sun. However, she had assured him on the phone last night that she was as good as new and anxious to get back to work. He reached into the back of the car and lifted out a huge sheaf of red roses and a bottle of champagne. Then, still whistling, he crossed the road and ran up the steps to the front door.

He was about to press the doorbell when he heard footsteps behind him and turned quickly. At the bottom of the steps stood Nick, carrying an enormous box of chocolates and a spray of exquisite white orchids. For a long moment they looked at each other in silence. Then Stone found himself smiling.

'Well, come on then,' he said. 'What are you waiting for?'

Upstairs in the window of Leo's sitting-room James Pascoe, already well down his first gin and tonic, watched the little encounter with some amusement.

'Leo?' he said.

She looked up from lighting the tall, pink candles on the dining-table. Dressed in a softly flowing white dress, her skin and hair burnished gold by the Aegean sun, she had regained all the heart stopping beauty that had made her famous.

'Yes, James?'

'You never did tell me—which one turned out to be Batman?'

She returned to her task, her smile deepening.

'Do you know,' she said thoughtfully, 'I still haven't made up my mind—but I'm working on it!'

*

Printed in Great Britain
by Amazon